Bedtime Stories for Adults

Relaxing Deep Sleep Hypnosis. Reduce Anxiety, Stress, Depression, and Insomnia. Mindfulness to Heal Your Brain.
Book 1

document, including, but not limited to, — errors, omissions, or inaccuracies.

Table of Contents

Introduction

Have you ever been lying in bed at night, staring at your ceiling and wishing that sleep would come for you? Maybe you were stuck there, desperate for that sleep to arrive, but no matter what you did, it was impossible. Your mind continued to race, and you couldn't slow it down. Insomnia strikes when we least expect it, and it can have all sorts of sources. Commonly, it is found in those suffering from anxiety and depression. However, just because you are suffering from that doesn't mean that you have to lose out on your sleep as well. Are you stressed out? Are you tired? Worried about the world? In a world filled with as many unpredictable variables, that comes as little surprise. However, we can overcome it.

Ultimately, if you are currently suffering from anxiety, depression, or even struggling from insomnia for reasons unknown to you, you are strongly encouraged to talk to your doctor. There may be underlying causes that this book will not be able to address. However, you can learn to begin mitigating the symptoms. This book is here to help you alleviate your insomnia through the use of mindfulness. It is not a cure, but it is a way that you can find some support for yourself if you need it, and it is here if you want to make use of it.

At the beginning of this book, you will be treated to seven short, slice of life stories that are there to be relaxing. They are designed to help to draw you into these worlds where your own personal worries can

begin to melt away. Through listening, you will realize
that you are at ease and at peace. As you read through
these, you will be following Sophie, a young, relatable
woman who doesn't quite know what she wants in life.
As you read her slice of life stories, you will watch her
enjoy herself, solve minor problems, and, more
importantly, find ways to relax and enjoy the moment
with those that live around her.

Then, as this book comes to a close, you will be treated
to two guided meditations. They are there to provide
you with a calming guide into that state of
mindfulness. As you follow the instructions, you will
feel your mind, your body, and your spirit beginning
to relax. You will feel your worries fade away and your
stress dissipate. They will gently ease you into a
receptive and calm state so that you will be able to
focus on the story and eventually fall asleep. These
two meditations should help you begin to relax just
enough that you feel far more receptive to that state of
sleep that you have been yearning for, and hopefully,
you will find that you can rest well.

Each and every story is designed to be compelling to
slowly lull you into that state of mindfulness so you
can focus on the story provided. Mindfulness is a state
of quiet, calming awareness. It is a state where you
can simply be in the moment. You let go of your
judgment, your worries, and your discomfort in favor
of being able to release the struggles that come with
them. You are able to heal yourself from the inside
out, defeating those negative thoughts that are
probably holding yourself back. As you do so, you find

that you are in peace with yourself. You find that you are content at the moment. You find that you are comfortable as the person that you are.

It might seem strange to listen to these stories to try to help yourself fall asleep, but they are there to be a gentle guide for you. They are designed to be something that you can rely on to better yourself, to feel calmer and more content in yourself as you head into this process. They will guide you into that calming state so that you can be certain that you are calm and ready to go.

Before you begin, however, there are a few key skills that you will need that will be addressed in the first few stories. These will come up in the meditative bedtime stories that you hear. You will need to know how to use mindful breathing to guide yourself into focusing on the right state of mind. You will need to use calm breathing to help yourself settle down. This works because it triggers your vagus nerve, which reminds your body to settle down. Deep breathing changes the pressure in your chest, and as a result, your vagus nerve reminds you to slow down. Your heart rate slows, and your blood pressure will settle down. Your stress hormones will begin to lower, and you will feel at peace. This is the key to relaxation before these stories, and it will take you far. You will also need to understand the idea of a body scan and how to perform them. Finally, you will need to understand what an affirmation is.

Mindful Breathing

Mindful breathing is the act of being able to breathe mindfully. It is to focus on your breaths as they come in and out without worry. When you do this, you are to focus entirely on your breathing without exception. Typically, this is done with one long breath in through the nose, usually for about five seconds. Then, you breathe out through your mouth. You do this more and more in order to calm yourself down. The purpose of mindful breathing is to focus entirely upon your breath without anything else. Every time that your thoughts drift from your breath, you gently and without judgment, push your attention back to it.

Body Scan

A body scan is a meditative technique where you go over your whole body, place by place. Usually, you start at your toes or your head and slowly work to the other end, stopping your awareness at each of the different areas of your body. Every part of you should be focused on one at a time before you move to the next. This is often joined with relaxing each part as you do so, but other times, it is simply becoming aware of the feelings at the moment in every part of your body.

Affirmations

Affirmations are a repetition of speech that is used to remind you of the critical points that you will need to remember. They are to help you to find calmness, peace, or even just to keep your mind focused on something that you are pursuing. When you use affirmations, the idea is that you are able to focus entirely on the moment on making something true. If you want to create your own affirmations for anxiety, stress, or depression to help yourself to manage them, you would repeat these phrases to yourself to sort of ground yourself at the moment. They should be personal, positive, and present-oriented so you can assert that they are true in their moment.

Ultimately, those are the most important aspects that you will need moving forward as you read through this book. You should find that you get plenty of information through doing so, and you should find that the process is simple enough. For the best impact, consider following along with a guided meditation to help yourself begin to relax so you can then move on to reading the stories if you are still awake. Hopefully, by the end of it, you will feel your own personal insomnia start to melt away. So, sit back, relax, get ready for bed, and let's begin!

Story 1: The Path Less Traveled

Sophie heads out for a nice, leisurely hike through the mountains with her German shepherd, Bella. However, things take a turn for the worst when she heads down the wrong road. Will Sophie learn to embrace the road less traveled and appreciate the beauty, or is she going to find herself miserable the entire time she tries to find her way back to the trail?

Beep! Beep! Beep!

"I'm up! I'm up!" shouted Sophie as she sat up, unceremoniously, in her bed. Her long, dark brown hair was all over the place as she pushed herself up, and next to her, Bella gave her what Sophie could only describe as a dubious look. Bella's black ears were cocked to the side, and she almost looked like she was raising an eyebrow at the utter lack of grace that Sophie had exhibited pushing herself up. She had practically tumbled out of bed entirely!

Sophie stuck a hand out to swat at the beeping alarm clock on her nightstand, blinking blearily. It had been yet another long night of struggling to sleep, and now that she had heard the alarm, she knew that she would never get back to sleep, no matter how exhausted she was. The clock's LED face was shining exactly 6:03 AM as she stared at it, and she sighed. As much as the appeal of bed was begging her to get back under the covers, she knew that it would be for the best if she

got up and out of bed. She swung her feet over the edge and patted Bella on the head.
"Well, Bells, what do you say we go hiking?"

Just the word "go" had led to the pup's ears to perk up even more, and she sat up with a doggy grin, mouth agape and tongue lolling out the side as she waited for her owner to actually get up and get moving. After all, Sophie wasn't always the most motivated person. 27 years old, still single, and working as a freelance article writer for her local newspaper, Sophie wasn't what most people would call conventionally all together, especially at her age. However, she also knew that she wasn't driven to follow the main path through life. Her path may be unconventional, but she was still fond of where life was taking her. Sure, most of her girlfriends were off getting married, buying houses, and settling down to have kids, but she still had years to think about that—she was more interested in enjoying life. Besides, no one she met ever seemed to enjoy her lackadaisical attitude, so why bother settling down if they aren't going to appreciate her in the first place?

Within an hour, bellies were full, bags were packed, and Sophie was taking Bella into the passenger seat, buckling her harness in, and then hopping into the driver's seat. With the music on and nursing another coffee the whole way there, they made their way out of town and up toward the local state park. The park itself was just outside of town, thankfully, but felt so isolated where it was. It was up at the edge of the foothills, and the park itself was miles and miles of winding trails through a massive forest. It was usually a pretty popular hiking destination, but something about 6 AM on a Wednesday morning seemed to clear it out well. After all, it was work time for most of the population. Sophie smiled to herself. She knew that she was lucky to have an unconventional schedule that meant that she had no competition when it came to doing things. Errands to run? She could run them during business hours while most people were at work or school. Is it an opening day for a popular movie? She could get the matinee showing and be one of maybe ten people in the theater. It certainly had its perks to be out and about during those business hours, and she could not deny the value.

Just as quickly as Sophie and Bella had hopped into the car, they hopped out and stood at the trailhead. "What do you think, Bells?" she asked, glancing down. Bella was standing next to her, perfectly obediently. The German shepherd looked up at her and met her gaze for a moment, tail swishing lazily behind her back. *Of course, you didn't answer,* Sophie found herself telling herself, mentally rolling her eyes. What did she expect? If she wanted a chatty hiking buddy, she would have had to wait for the weekend to go with a friend or something.

Rather than bothering to waste the mental energy on thinking about that, she looked up at the trail instead. The forest was a vibrant green—almost too green to be real, and yet there it was right in front of her. It was beautiful as it stretched out and up the hillside. The trees grew together so densely that the entire forest was deeply shaded. Very little of the sunlight actually managed to filter through the verdant foliage, but Sophie preferred it that way, anyway. She was pale and had a tendency to burn, so the added protection of the shade was a net positive for her.

Off they began, walking through the trail. As soon as they rounded the first bend, it was like they had been transported to a whole new world. Without a clear line of sight to the parking lot that she had left her car in, it was like they were really engulfed in the wilderness. The trees grew so thickly that any sounds of people were drowned out. All she could hear above and around them were the sounds of hundreds of birds chirping away that fine morning.

She knew that they were flitting about—they were all over the place. Occasionally, the sound of rustling feathers would cut through the melodies of their songs, and the quick blur of a bird darting across their path would grace their view. It was utterly peaceful as they walked. The trail, though somewhat rough and steep at times, wasn't too difficult to get through, and she could see that Bella was having a great time. The pup was happily walking alongside her, tail wagging and without so much as pulling.

As they walked, Sophie found herself getting lost in her mind. She watched the trail in front of her, simply letting her mind wander from place to place. It was easy to let herself get lost in thought as she walked. It was peaceful to simply allow her thoughts to drift endlessly. The more that she did so, the more she felt like she was calm. Being in nature had that effect for her—the more that she wandered about inside of it, the more at ease she felt like she was. The ground underfoot felt somewhat soft, she realized as she continued along.

Soon, Bella and Sophie found themselves at a cross-section. She looked to the left and to the right. Neither trail was marked, and she was unsure which was the right way. "You know," she murmured to herself thoughtfully, running a hand through her hair, "I'm pretty sure that Emma from work told me that if we took a right at the fork, we'd end up heading right back to the parking lot. She said it was a loop or something." She looked left, and then right once more, and then set down on the path. "It's only a mile or so back to the car... So we should be there in the next twenty minutes?"

This path was markedly denser than the one that they had been walking down—it was much more crowded with trees, and the further they walked, the thinner the trail itself seemed to get. She looked around, seeing that even the trees seemed to change—though before, they had been mostly around trees with soft leaves, it seemed like the further they went, the more the trees shifted into being more pine instead. They were beautiful, and the scent of sap and soft earth filled the air, but Sophie found herself worrying a bit.

"It's probably nothing, right?" she told herself, shaking off that doubt. She didn't want to give up on that gorgeous trail just because of that nagging feeling that they were going the wrong way. Bella simply wagged her tail in return, perfectly content to be walking about in the forest.

To help herself pass the time as they walked, Sophie turned her attention to her breathing. It was ragged as their path slowly became much more uphill suddenly. Strange, she thought to herself—why would it go uphill when they were supposed to be heading back to the parking lot?

Then, it dawned on her: They weren't heading to the parking lot at all. They were going deeper into the woods. Sophie stopped in her tracks, arms hanging limply at her sides, and she looked at Bella in disbelief. "Bells!" she announced incredulously. "What happened to that master sniffer of yours?!" She rubbed at Bella's head and groaned, and the German shepherd licked her hand as if trying to make her feel better about the situation. She looked around herself and realized that she had no idea where they were, and she had turned several times since getting to that point. She had no idea how they were going to get back to the car.

Pulling out her phone revealed no signal, so using GPS wasn't exactly an option. She also didn't have a printout of the map of the area, nor would that have helped since she had no clue where she was at that point in time. She looked around and sighed. It was just her luck to end up lost. What if she was lost forever? What if a bear found her? Or worse, a serial killer? The thoughts raced through her head, and she

felt herself break out in a cold sweat, goosebumps
breaking out across her arms as the hair on the back
of her neck stood on edge. Suddenly, that peaceful
getaway in the mountains was anything but.

"Get a grip!" she told herself firmly, forcing herself to
take a deep breath. "There are no bears here, and
they're certainly aren't any serial killers," she told
herself feebly as if to convince herself through sheer
willpower. It didn't work. She breathed deeply, in and
out, and looked around the area. If they had been
hiking up, going deeper and deeper into the park, then
the logical answer was to head back down toward the
foot of the hill, right?

Tightening her grip around Bella's leash, Sophie took
in a deep breath and turned around. "No big deal,"
she told herself. "Just gotta backtrack!" And so, she
set off, heading back down the mountain. At the very
least, it was easy to tell when she was going down
based on the slope.

Before long, however, she felt like she was even more
lost than before. But, this time, she heard something
other than the sounds of the birds or the wind rustling
the leaves. It was the sound of gently bubbling water
over rocks, not far from where they were. It sounded
incredibly close. What a relief, she told herself as she
looked for the source. She remembered that there was
a creek not too far from where they had parked—
perhaps this source of water would lead to it. She
moved her way through the woods carefully, trudging
through the path with determination. She wasn't

willing to allow the fear at the moment to keep her from getting back down the mountain, and off she went, heading toward the sound.

It didn't take long before the trees separated to give way to a beautiful little creek. It wasn't much—maybe three feet across and just a few inches deep, but it was a welcome sight after so much wandering about aimlessly. Bella barked once and wagged her tail, looking up at Sophie with pleading eyes. She wanted to splash in the water a bit, and quite frankly, Sophie couldn't blame her. She wanted to do the same thing. Her feet were starting to get sore too. She slid her shoes off, quickly discarding them and her socks to the side, and took a step into the cool water.

The water was chilly at first, and she gasped at the sudden shift of temperature before breaking out into a big grin. Bella pounced into the water too, happily splashing about with her large paws. Her tail wagged furiously, sending droplets of water splattering everywhere. The rocks in the water were smooth, worn down over the years of water running over them. They were gentle under her feet, and she was thankful for that. She was thankful for a whole lot at the moment. Turning around to look around her, she saw that there was so much more to see. She could see that the trees, though verdant and green, were also standing tall. Their branches were intertwined together as they stretched together, blocking out the sun. Occasionally, she could see the quick glimpse of beautiful, crystal-clear sky shining behind the leaves, only for it to fade away behind another leaf.

It was beautiful, and at that moment, as the cool water gently caressed her toes and lapped up against her ankles, Sophie was at peace. Suddenly, her troubles melted away. She was there, in that moment, privy to a beautiful scene of trees that were thriving, with a clean creek of water. She was there with her dog, loving the moment, and she found herself so happy to be there in the moment. Yes, it had been a struggle to get there, and yes, it wasn't where she was heading to originally, it was still worth it in the end.

She smiled down at Bella and patted her on the head, and Bella returned the gesture with a puppy grin. They spent just one more moment lingering there, taking in the peaceful moment. The birds continued to sing. The trees continued to rustle together, creating a beautiful percussion behind the sounds of the trees.

Bella barked loudly and pounced at something in the water.

And just as suddenly as the moment of peace came, it was gone.

Sophie turned her attention just in time to see Bella chasing after a frog that was swimming as quickly as it could downstream. "Bella!!" she cried out with a grin in faux exasperation. "Leave it!" Laughing, she tugged at the leash to guide Bella out of the water. She dried off her feet with a spare towel she kept in her hiking pack and slid her socks and shoes back on. They followed the creek, and sure enough, it brought them right back to the parking lot that they had been in.

Disaster averted!

When they were settled into the car, Sophie let herself flop against the back of the seat and sigh. Though she was mentally at ease and feeling recharged, her entire body, every fiber of her being was exhausted and ready for a nice, long nap as soon as they got home. She was ready to cash in on that extra sleep that she had been wanting but putting off, and by the looks of Bella, who quickly curled up, somehow not falling off of the seat, the sentiment was shared.

Story 2: Airport Antics

It's vacation time! Sophie is ready to head out to the airport to travel to Greece with her good friend, Cara. But, she has to get there in time! Sophie's got to move quickly if she wants to make it to the airport and onto her flight on time to enjoy the vacation of her dreams, but everything seems to be working against her. Will she make it to the terminal on time?

It was a surprisingly drizzly day on that fine morning. The sky was overcast, swollen with the threat of rain ahead of what would be a busy day. The sun was completely obscured, and the darkened sky sort of lingered over everything. It was definitely not the bright, cheery day that it should have been, and it almost made everything seem a bit less exciting than she felt like it should have been. She was thrilled—in less than six hours, she would be on a plane headed to Greece—but she had to get there first, and it was looking like it would be a long day full of more than she expected.

Sophie sipped at her coffee as she looked out the window over her lawn. It was quite flat back there, with the occasional hole dug out by Bella, and without her trusty German shepherd running about, it felt almost empty out there. But, Bella had been left with Sophie's mother the night prior so she'd be supervised during the vacation. After all, Sophie had a feeling that if she had left the pup to her own devices all alone for a week, she would be returning to utter destruction throughout the entire house, and that was not something that she was really interested in dealing with at that point in time. Who had time to clean up all of the torn-up carpets that a bored dog would inevitably leave behind?

As Sophie finished up her last sips of coffee, she turned her attention to the list written on the purple sticky note sitting on her table. Along the lines, in bubbly letters, she had written her to-do list for the day:

- *Pack carry-on bag*
- *Fill automatic plant waterers*
- *Make sure ALL lights are off*
- *Put passport in purse*
- *Lock door*

It wasn't much of a long list, but all week long, she had forgotten to pick up her passport from her drawer. She kept forgetting all about it, and she knew that if she made it to the airport without her passport, all bets would be off. She'd let herself down, she'd miss her plane, and both she and Cara would be miserable. She couldn't do that to everyone! She really wanted to make sure that the entire vacation was as easy as possible to get through so they could have as much fun as possible. That meant making sure that everything on her end was as impeccably managed as it could be, and she was determined not to leave anything up to chance or fate—she was determined to make sure that everything about her trip was perfect.

It didn't take long for her to knock everything off her list, and that was with even remembering to slip her passport right into place in her purse as well, next to her phone and her keys. Just as she finished making sure that her purse had everything she needed all packed up, she heard a knock at the door before it opened up.

"Hell-oooo!" she heard cried out in a falsetto downstairs, and she grinned in response.

"I'm upstairs!" Sophie called back from her room, not even bothering to poke her head downstairs to see her friend downstairs. She closed up her purse and looked to the clothes that she had lined up on her bed. She had picked out a cute flowy skirt that hit her knees, made of ruffled material in a bright, floral yellow print. It was definitely on the side of bohemian casual, especially when paired with her white off-the-shoulder top. It was comfortable, breezy, and plenty flexible so she wouldn't be miserable as she sat on the plane. After all, from their local airport to Athens was roughly 13 hours, not counting loading, getting off the plane, getting through customs, or anything else. It was going to be exhausting—but hopefully worth it to have that time to unwind.

Cara poked her head into the door to Sophie's room and looked shocked at what she saw. "Sophie!!" she gasped in shock. "Surely you're not going like that, honey. That will... Not do. Not at all!" With a sigh, Cara stormed right into the room, shaking her head and tutting her disapproval. "Honey, how many times have I told you? No white after Labor Day!" She rushed into the room, her blonde hair bouncing behind her in perfectly groomed waves. Cara was, as she liked to refer to it, as a "connoisseur of fashion," and her wardrobe definitely screamed as such. Even today, she was wearing a strappy dress in black with geometric circles patterning across it in white. Around her waist was a thin black belt, tucking in and showing off her curves. Over her shoulders was a small, black blazer with ¾ sleeves. On her feet were two heeled, strappy sandals in shiny black leather, and she was walking around with a strappy black purse draped over her shoulder.

"What's wrong with white after Labor Day?" Sophie replied with a frown, looking down at the clothing hanging from her body. "I thought I looked great!"

"Yeah, maybe if you're just heading down the street for your morning coffee before you get ready for the day... You're going to ATHENS, BABY!! Dress the part!" With a dramatic flair of her arm, Cara tossed the bag onto the bed and immediately stepped into Sophie's walk-in closet, looking around for something. She rummaged around in the clothing, muttering to herself under her breath. Sophie rubbed the back of her head sheepishly as she waited around, catching only some of the quiet tirade that Cara was going on about. "No... No.... Not enough... Wrong..."

"You know, I think it'll be fine..." Sophie told her with a quick peek into the closet, but just as she put her

head into the door to see what was going on, she had a
bunch of clothing thrown right at her.

"No, it will not be fine! Be *civilized,* Sophie!" Cara
tutted again as she walked out, looking at her
handiwork that was currently draped over Sophie's
face and shoulder. Cara had chosen out a casual dress
made of navy fabric with a deep V cut down the
neckline. It was held up by two straps over the
shoulder, and the fabric had a pretty print of pale pink
flowers growing across it. The dress was narrow at the
waist and flared out toward the hemline, creating a
bouncy swing to it when it was worn. "Wear this one!"

Sophie shrugged her shoulders. It really didn't matter
that much to her, but if Cara cared, she'd deal with it
anyway. She tugged her shirt and skirt and then put
on the dress. The fabric was smooth as it gently clung
to her waist and hugged in all the right places, and she
loved the feeling. The shoes, white pumps, were
pulled on with it, and she picked up her purse. "Fine,
fine, ready?" she asked Cara, who clapped her hands
and squealed in delight before heading down the
stairs head of Sophie.

"I'll be waiting outside!"

Sophie nodded and looked out the window. It was still
overcast and looked like rain would start at any point.
Briefly, she wondered if what she was wearing would
even be enough in the moment. Could she really wear
that in the rain? "Well... I'll be inside most of the day.
It'll be fine." She pulled her purse over her shoulder

and ran down the stairs and out the door, locking the door behind her. She was ready!

Cara was already sitting outside in her shiny silver Prius, car running to warm up. The first drops of rain were beginning to fall. As Sophie dragged out her luggage and loaded it up in the trunk, she looked at the time—they had an hour to get to the airport and another two to get through customs and boarded onto their flight. Thankfully, their airport was only precisely 52 minutes away, according to GPS, and they'd be able to get there rather quickly—they'd just have to hope that traffic agreed with them.

With both of them in the car and ready to go, Cara was off. The rain picked up quickly as they went down the road, and Cara groaned. "We're going to be late…" she mused as she ran a hand through her hair and looked over her shoulder as she switched lanes on the interstate, dipping into the carpool lane in hopes of shaving off even a few minutes. Glancing at the clock, Sophie could see her doing mental math as she tried to calculate just how quickly above traffic speed she'd have to go if she wanted to get to the airport with any time to spare.

The rain was harder now, thudding against the roof of the car like drums as they drove. In the distance, they could hear a summer thunderstorm rumbling away, and occasionally, the sky, far from them, would flash for a moment. "What a day for a storm!" Sophie said as she looked out the window listlessly, chin resting on her hand and her other hand resting on her lap.

She watched the rain drifting off the window absently as traffic slowed to a crawl. As the rain picked up, driving conditions continued to drop, and soon, it felt like it would be too dangerous to keep going at that rate. They had to slow down, or they would have been in an accident.

But then traffic fell to a standstill. Cara slammed her hand against the car's steering wheel. "We're going to be late!" she growled under her breath, leaning over to try to peer ahead of the car in front of her. Traffic was barely moving at all, and her GPS was reporting that there had been an accident not too far from where they were at that moment. "What are we going to do?" she lamented, glancing over at Sophie.

"Well..." Sophie began, deliberating over her words as she looked over at her friend. Cara looked incredibly stressed out at the moment—her eyes were wide, and her lips were tense. "We'll be okay. I'm sure they'll be able to clear the accident quickly, and we'll be on our way in no time."

"I hope you're right," Cara sighed as she slumped against her seat, letting her hands fall off the steering wheel. She turned up the music a bit, and gentle music played in the background, not really exciting enough to catch their attention, but it also made the car's silence just a bit more tolerable as the rain continued to pound, harder still this time.

"I am," Sophie said with a resolute nod, though the waver in her voice betrayed her nervousness. Still, she had to be strong—she had to be convincing enough for the both of them. Of course, she was not quite convinced anyhow—it was hard for her to believe that they would make it on time with the slowdown, especially when they heard the sirens approaching, and the ambulance and fire truck made their way past them to presumably where the accident had occurred. They could see the flashing lights ahead, so it must have been incredibly close to where they were. Had they left a few minutes earlier, they probably would have been caught in it. At the very least, she told herself, they were safe. They hadn't been hurt, and if the worst thing that happened to them was that they missed their flight and had to book the next one, then their days were still going better than the people who had been in that accident. Their inconvenience was better than the pain that would be felt in an accident.

Traffic slowly began to move, crawling through just one lane that they were able to merge into slowly. They crept along until they finally passed the wreckage. A red SUV's front was crumpled in, and the other car, a small silver sedan, was slammed into the concrete divider to the left of the freeway. EMTs were tending to people who were all sitting up, looking shaken up but ultimately, okay as they passed.

"Wow..." Cara breathed out as she glanced at the accident. She was uncharacteristically at a loss for words as she looked at the scene. It looked awful. Both cars were almost certainly a total loss.

"They're lucky..." Sophie whispered as she eyed the carnage. Aside from being shaken up, it looked like everyone was doing okay, especially since both ambulances that had passed them earlier were still there, doors open, with the paramedics doing rounds between the people. Both Sophie and Cara fell silent, radio still gently playing the music and rain still thundering on the roof.

The rest of the drive to the airport happened in relative silence with just the melodies coming from the speakers and the cadence of the rain rapping at the roof. Cara was driving notably more carefully as they made their way there, and though they were running a few minutes late, that scene seemed to give her pause when it came to rushing through the rain. It certainly was not the weather to be trying to speed across the street.

Before long, they made it to the airport and got parked. They were still two and a half hours before their flight would leave—giving them plenty of time to get through customs. They dragged along their luggage behind them as they walked through the rain, with Cara holding an umbrella precariously in one hand while trying to pull two-wheeled luggage containers behind her.

Entering the airport was the easy part. What came next, the constant waiting, was the worst of it. They had to wait in line to check-in, causing Cara to tap absently at the handle to her black luggage. Sophie tugged at a strand of hair, curling it around her hair as

she people watched. There were all sorts of people out
and about, and they were all going in a different
direction. Some were dressed for sheer comfort,
wearing sweats and a t-shirt while others were
dressed for business, prim, and proper. It was
interesting to see all of the different people going in,
as well as seeing the people of all walks of life going
out as well. Some of them were clearly foreigners,
rubbing heads and speaking in different languages as
they looked around in confusion and attempted to
piece together English sentences just enough to get a
cab while others were eagerly following their tour
guides who seemed ready to take them to wherever
they were planning to head first. There were some
groups of young adults as well—likely college students
heading out for spring vacation.

The people-watching was always Sophie's favorite part
of being at an airport, and it helped her to pass the
time. She'd imagine all of the different situations
behind the different people. She'd start imagining
whole lives for these people. She'd think about the
people's vacation plans as they came into town. She
imagined that they'd go to all the famous tourist sites
in town—they'd go and see the restaurants and the
beach as well. She assumed that they'd all have a
grand time, looking over the city in their hotel rooms,
or that they'd be spending time at a rental home.

Before long, she felt Cara tapping her back to the real
world, snapping her out of her reverie. "Ready?" she
asked Sophie, who blinked in surprise. She hadn't
realized that she had been spending so much of her

time just thinking about other things, and she nodded her head, pulling out her passport and letting the attendant see it.

Checking in and handing in the luggage was simple—then it was time to wait for boarding. They went through the security gates and stood in line at the boarding gate for their plane. The line was already quite long, and they still had another 30 minutes to boarding.

"Are you ready?" Sophie asked Cara as she fiddled with her purse strap, grinning at her friend.

"Oh, am I!" Cara echoed with a thumbs up. "I'm so ready!"

"Same! Greece, here we come!" Sophie was thrilled—she was so ready to go through the different sights they had to see. She wanted to see the ruins of Acropolis and get to eat all of the god food. She was thrilled about the beach that they'd get to go visit, and being able to go through it all on their own was something that was thrilling to her—she was so ready to be able to go through it all. Her dream as a child had always been to go to Greece, and she was finally living that chance.

Before long, the line to board was moving, and they were in their seats. They had first-class seats, at Cara's insistence. Once they were on the plane, they realized that it was absolutely worth it as well—the seats were massively luxurious, comfortable, and absolutely worth every cent that Cara had so generously paid.

The seatbelt light came on, and the voice of the flight attendant came on the overhead, informing everyone of the rules, regulations, and what to expect, and before they knew it, they were up in the air, high above the world beneath them and heading toward the open ocean.

Cara and Sophie toasted to each other with the complimentary glass of wine that they were each given. "To safe travels!" they said as their glasses clinked together. They both sipped and laughed at each other. It was going to be a long flight—but at least it was a flight in luxury!

Story 3: Acropolis

Sophie and Cara have made it to Greece on their vacation, and after their resting day to catch up on all the missed sleep, they are ready to get going and finally start exploring. This day is Sophie's turn to choose what they do for the day, and she has chosen to explore the Acropolis of Athens, getting a glimpse at the past first hand.

Sophie yawned as she rolled out of bed. She was in one room of the two-room suite that Cara had insisted upon for their vacation, and so far, she loved every moment of the luxury. The flooring was a soft, plush carpet that squished so comfortably underneath her feet, almost just as invitingly as the bed had gently squished underneath her as well. The suite was overlooking the gulf to the south of Athens, and her window gave her a beautiful, breathtaking view of the bright, clear water. Across the sea, she could see land gently rolling toward the horizon as well, and there were tiny, bright sails lit up all around the water. It was a wonderful start to the morning; she told herself as she looked out at the view.

She watched for another few minutes before taking a shower in a wonderful stall, carefully tiled with beautiful marble. Getting ready in luxury was a breeze, and she was utterly relaxed as she washed the last of the soap through her hair. She was up early—her night-owl nature was really helping her out during the travels—jetlag meant that she was perfectly content being up in the daylight hours since she already normally was awake at that time, relative to her home, anyway.

Stepping out, she was greeted by a plush robe that she wrapped herself in to dry off, and she brewed a coffee using the small machine provided in her hotel room. The wondrous scent of coffee filled the air, waking her up more as it brewed. It smelled roasted and comforting—a bit of familiarity in her travels abroad, and she was thrilled to have that opportunity afforded to her in the first place. She was thrilled that her time was going to be spent enjoying the moment and actually having some peace and quiet to herself for a while. It was nice being able to take her time without waking up and immediately rushing to her computer to look over everything. It was nice being able to simply go throughout her day without being so overly concerned with everything that she was doing at any given point in time. It was enjoyable being able to go through her morning routine in leisure at her own speed.

By the time that she had finished up her coffee, she noticed that Cara had finished getting herself ready as well. She stepped out of her own room in a nice, airy blue dress that gently clung to her waist, and half of her hair tied up and back, out of her face. She wore tan strapped sandals that somehow managed to be the perfect blend of functional and attractive at the same time, and her black sunglasses were carefully perched atop her head. Her makeup was impeccably done, perfectly put on while still somehow managing to capture that natural look to it as well. She looked great. Even on vacation and even when their itinerary for the day involved walking, she still managed to look wonderful. It was a wonder she was still single, Sophie marveled as she looked on toward her friend. "You're not ready yet?" Cara asked, raising a perfectly sculpted eyebrow up in surprise.

Sophie grinned back. "I'm enjoying taking my time for a change! I'll be ready to go in a few minutes." All she really had left to do was get dressed, and she'd be good to go, too. She wasn't nearly as particular about her looks as Cara tended to be. So, while Cara sipped at her own coffee on the balcony overlooking the gulf, Sophie got ready to go. She tossed on some khaki high-waisted shorts that came just above her knees and a white chiffon top, tucked into the waistband. She was comfortable, yet functional as she also tied on her walking shoes and picked up the wide-brimmed hat that she placed atop her head. She walked out to meet Cara, waving for her to follow.

Cara stood up and put away her cup. "That looks quaint," she acknowledged with a smile.

"Thanks," Sophie said, choosing to take the comment as a compliment rather than bothering to say a word about it. She grinned and bounced as they walked down the hall together. She was brimming with excitement—heading to visit Acropolis had been one of her lifelong dreams that she had for herself, and she was finally living it! She was so happy to do so, and even though she knew that it would be crowded and nothing like it once was, there was something thrilling about going somewhere that was built nearly 2500 years ago. Though it was beginning to crumble, it was a real testament to the power of humanity, even that long ago.

Sophie was incredibly impressed with what she had seen in the books—every time she ever looked at the pictures of the ruins, it was gorgeous—tall, crumbling, and flawed, but that made it so much more awe-inspiring to view. It was made before humanity had levels and laser pointers to help them measure our angles just right. They built them before people had machines to help lift these massive behemoths of stone and marble. They were so immaculately and impeccably carved for people that only had their hands and small hand tools to work with, and she couldn't help but be fascinated with them. She loved being able to explore them, to learn about the world around her, and to learn how to better begin to relate to how people used to live.

Cara might not enjoy exploring around as much as the shopping and the sightseeing, but for Sophie, being able to see just how humanity used to live was so worth every moment of travel that came with it. She didn't particularly enjoy flying, but getting to go around all of the different historical sites gave her a great perspective over everything and everyone involved.

Stepping outside of the hotel had them immediately hit with warm, humid air that smelled of the beach and of promise for a day of fantastic exploration and sightseeing. It smelled of excitement and of being able to meet those lifelong goals once and for all, and Sophie was entirely ready to throw herself into it all. Even Cara, who was typically uninterested in such events and fun, had a smile on her face as they walked out. Even though Cara had a tendency to be very set in her ways, she had a huge soft spot for making sure that her dear friend was happy, and this day was no exception to that matter. She was willing to put on a happy face to go through everything with her friend if it meant seeing Sophie's dream come true.

"Did you know that Acropolis is referred to as the crowning jewel of Greece, *and* it is the birthplace of democracy?" Sophie practically squealed as she walked through the path. "It's such an important site! AND, even though it was damaged, it is still there for us to see now."

"Really?" Cara asked in return. It was hard not to feel excited when she watched Sophie bubbling over the words that were being said. She grinned back at her friend. It was always pleasant to see just how worked up Sophie would get when she was talking about something she loved. "What happened to it anyway?"

"What, with the damage?"

"Yeah. It's pretty broken down now, isn't it?" Cara replied as they made their way to the site.

"It is! So back during the Morean War, the war between the Turkish and Venice, Acropolis held the gunpowder that they would use. But, during a battle in 1687, the Parthenon, the main building that everyone thinks about when they're thinking of the Acropolis, was hit with a cannonball. When that happened, it kind of all blew up! And now, it has that broken down look that it had. But, there's more to Acropolis than just the Parthenon, too. It was a great big citadel built atop a big hill. It was called acropolis because it is so high—did you know that acro means extreme or high, while polis means city? It's high up in the city, and the one in Athens is the most popular." Sophie was bouncing along with every step as she talked away. She knew her Greek history and mythology and was not afraid to show it off.

"Wow, that's... A lot of a lot!" Cara said, patting Sophie on the shoulder. "But I'm really excited to go see everything. It should look great."

"Me too!" Sophie squealed.

It didn't take them long to arrive at the location where their tour bus would pick them up, and they waited among the small crowd of people, happily chatting. The Acropolis was in the center of the city, overlooking everything around it. It had once been the home of some of the most important parts of the city, dedicated to Athena, the patron of the city, and it was an incredibly popular tourist site year-round. This meant two things: One, that they would have to be around lots of people, but two, that they would be able

to get to the site without having to walk all across
Athens.
The bus was filled up, and before they knew it, they
were being addressed by the tour guide. He was a tall,
thin young man with beautiful olive skin. His hair was
trimmed at the sides and slicked back, and his face
was impeccably sculpted. His eyes were kind as he
talked to them, and he appeared to be genuinely
passionate about his heritage as he spoke to them.

"Ooh, look at the eye candy," Cara said, nudging
Sophie on the bus with a sly smile on her face and
giggling.

Sophie looked at her with a scandalized expression.
"Shh!!" she shushed her friend, giggling quietly as
well. Cara was not wrong—he was a very handsome
man, and even better, he was telling them all about
everything that they would be learning about on the
tour. But, what he had to say was mostly just the same
details that Sophie had parroted about the entire walk
to the stop. He mentioned the history and what they
could expect, as well as some rules that they would all
have to follow to ensure that everything went
smoothly.

"The hill was picked out," he said through his Greek
accent, "Primarily because of the fact that it sat so
high up. It was the area where the locals settled down
to live, and the rock at the top was deemed where the
ruler would live. It was not until later that it gained
recognition as being associated with the goddess
Athena, and it was not until the 8th century. Athena

gained her own temple on the northeastern side of the hill." He looked around the tour bus, seeing that most of the people were only mildly interested at best. "But, the Parthenon is the most popular of all. It has withstood over the centuries, surviving fire, earthquakes, wars, and even explosions while still standing. It was once a powerful symbol of religion and culture of Athens, and today, it still endures, showing the true perseverance of the Greek people and of the Athenians themselves."

Sophie grinned at the man, glad to hear someone else sharing her passion for the history of such a magnificent building, but she was not interested in approaching him, even with Cara's incessant nudging. Yes, he was good looking, but she didn't really want to go through the hassle of an international fling, even if it were just a temporary ordeal. That didn't sound particularly appealing to her, even if they both shared a certain appreciation for the Greek culture.

Before long, they had arrived. The bus slowly squealed to a stop, and they all unloaded, one by one, to get off the bus. Then, Sophie got her first glance of it all. They were down toward the bottom of the rocky wall that built up the city. They were in for plenty of walking, but still, the sight was breathtaking. Against the blue sky, she could see the buildings, all aligned. The Parthenon's stark white walls and pillars clashed against the sky, and she could see that the line was already building up.

"This," the tour guide called out, pointing to the
entrance to the area, "is the path to the center of it all.
It is here that you will be able to follow the path that
thousands of years ago, the ancient people of Athens
walked when they entered this sacred area. This is the
road to the Parthenon, to the altar of Athena, and
more. As you enter, remember to remain respectful.
This area is ancient—it deserves the respect that you
would have in any ancient relic. It is a part of my
people's history, and if you cannot honor the rules.
Where you are standing right now is the gate to the
Acropolis, the Propylaia. It was here that people were
able to enter, and in order to pass through, in the time
when this sanctuary was dedicated to the great
Athena, only certain people were allowed to enter.
You must take nothing, and you must leave nothing
but your footsteps behind in this great, sacred place.
Now, are you ready?"

The group of people in the tour all gave a weak cheer
and chuckle, and off they went into the site. It was
beautiful, Sophie marveled as they finally took their
first steps in. The stones were surprisingly lightly
colored underneath her feet, and she looked up at the
eight massive pillars supporting the beam that
undoubtedly once made up the building's roof in front
of her. Sophie was practically bouncing in excitement
as they stood outside under the sun—she was thrilled
to see everything in front of her, and she was ready to
dive in. Of course, the tour had different plans.

As they toured the structures, they slowly traveled
from ruin to ruin. Their tour guide was happy to

explain to them everything that they would be doing and why he loved each and every building. He was quick to provide information about every single building.

The first stop was the Erechtheion, a temple located in the northern part of the Acropolis. As Sophie gazed upon the building's crumbling walls and the strange sculptures of women on one end, she listened closely. "The Porch of the Maidens," her tour guide begun, "Was added there to hide the beam that supports the southwest corner of the building. Due to budgeting constraints after the beginning of the Peloponnesian War, the building's size was cut, and as such, they had to find a way to disguise the pillar. Thus, the caryatids were built to create something beautiful to view and look at them!" All six women stood there, balancing the roof of the building on their heads, and yet, each and every single one looked graceful.

Before long, they had moved on to the Temple of Athena Nike. The massive temple stood tall on the stretch of land. It was built to provide a place to honor Athena Nike, the goddess of victory. It was a beautiful temple, complete with a beautiful carving of Athena herself trying to adjust the strap of a sandal.

They made it through several of the buildings, but the last one that they approached was the one that Sophie had been looking forward to the most: The Parthenon. "The Parthenon was created," the tour guide begun, "Primarily to provide people with a place to gather. It was the hubbub for all religious life in Athens, and the temple itself, built by Pericles, was believed to represent the power, lavish culture, and wealth that Athens enjoyed during the time. Today, it has remained one of the largest and most recognizable buildings that exist. It was eventually overtaken by the Byzantines after their conquering of Greece and was turned into a church. Then, again, it was converted when another empire, the Ottomans, took over Athens. It was converted then into a mosque. However, upon the war in 1687, the building was detonated when a cannonball from the Christian Holy League, attempting to reclaim their land, hit the ammunition depot and caused a detonation."

"Oh, so you were right!" Cara said with a grin.

"Shh!" Sophie hushed her as she marveled at the building. Though in ruins now, it was still magnificent to look on to. It was huge—a massive testament to human ability and skill, and something about it was absolutely amazing to behold. Her heart was happy— she had finally managed to check another item off her bucket list.

Story 4: Rainy Day Blues

One of the worst parts about living in the Pacific Northwest, Sophie had to admit, was the rain. Yes, it had its place. Yes, it was beautiful when she was inside, looking out at the vibrant green of the leaves and grass all around her. Yes, she felt like the luckiest woman out there to be able to live in such a beautiful, diverse, and welcoming area. But, she couldn't stand when the rain never relented.

On days when it rained, Sophie felt stuck. She felt like he had no choice but to stay indoors, and sometimes, she was simply restless. Sometimes, she just wanted to get outside and enjoy the day. Sometimes, she wanted to work on exercising her weary bones and body, and she wanted to find somewhere nice to do so. Of course, when it's constantly drizzling rain, it is hard to find somewhere comfortable to go jogging or to go hiking outdoors, and that constraint could be frustrating.

Sophie sighed as she sipped into her mug of tea. It was the cusp of autumn, and she could see it in the faintly yellowish tinge to the trees outside. It was on the slight chill that she felt in the air whenever she stepped outside, or the scent of leaves starting to die on the air. It was in the shortening of days and the lengthening of darkened mornings. It was in the fact that pumpkin spice was suddenly everywhere, even if it didn't always belong. It was something that brought the smell of cinnamon and spice or apple pies, but she couldn't help but sigh to herself. She loved summer. It was the short reprieve from the constant rain and drizzle that was all she could get in the area most of the year. It was the time when she got to really enjoy the weather and the climate, from kayaking on the lake to be able to hike through the mountains.

Next to her, Bella was curled up, fast asleep. She had done her business like normal, but rather than taking advantage of the time to go outside and play, she seemed more interested in sleeping more than anything else. Maybe the cold was getting to her too, Sophie mused as she took another sip of her tea before looking outside. Despite the ample watering, the grass on her back lawn was already starting to yellow, and there was not really anything that she could do about it but shrug and move on. It wouldn't be worth the hassle of trying to fight off the inevitable shift to winter.

With a sigh, Sophie finished up her tea and put the mug away. She knew that she had to work, but for some reason, she just couldn't bring herself to do so. She wanted to sit and enjoy the day, but to enjoy the day, she wanted sunlight and warmth. Unfortunately, the sky said it had vastly different plans, judging by the grey clouds, pregnant with rain, and ready to spill at a moment's notice. That meant that her original plan of walking through a local park known for its immaculate landscaping was out. She had been looking forward to looking at the different plants that were thriving in her area—she was hoping to figure out what she would plant in her own garden as she was pretty sick of looking at all of the grass all the time.

"I guess I could watch a movie..." she murmured under her breath as she stood up to wash her mug. But, a movie didn't sound very fun at all. She wasn't really interested in sitting around and watching what other people were doing. She was much more interested in finding a way to get moving. Even as she scrolled through the recent new additions on her streaming app on her phone, nothing stood out to her. She had seen most of the mainstream movies, and it didn't look like there was anything that was actually compelling or interesting to her in the theaters at that point in time either, so a movie was out, and honestly, she didn't mind at all.

Reading a book was usually her second pick, but she was feeling somewhat burnt out over reading after spending extra time reading over and editing some books on the side that she normally would not have been responsible for. She chose not to bother with reading at all, feeling that her eyes and mind needed a bit of a reprieve from written words for a while. After all, when you live and breathe writing at all times, you are bound to get bored.

Playing video games was out too—she had never really been one to play video games, and the idea of sitting around to do so was something that she had very little interest in, all things considered. She didn't even own a video game console in her home, nor did she care to do so.

She sighed again as she settled down into a cozy recliner in her living room, tucking her legs up and wrapping her arms around them. She was totally lost at what she should do with herself, and no amount of thinking seemed to be enough for her.

Pulling out her phone, she shot a quick text to several of her friends, but none of them seemed like they wanted to get together. With every rejection and every failed lead on something to do, Sophie sank deeper into her chair. It wasn't fun feeling like no one wanted to be around her, and in that moment, she was getting serious abandoned vibes and didn't know what she could do to make it better. She was stuck—she felt like she had no choice in the matter but to find something to do on her own since not even Bella seemed like she wanted to do anything.

Without a plan in mind, Sophie got up, went upstairs, and got dressed for the day. She was wearing the perfect transition to fall look for a dreary, drizzly, chilly day. Her top was a thin ombre sweater, starting with black around the hemline and sleeves and slowly fading into a purple, and finally, into a light grey. Throughout the sweater, there were other colors speckled into it as well. Her pants were a pair of dark blue skinny jeans, and on her feet were her trusty boots that she rarely ever went without in the winter and fall months—they were grey and up to her mid-calf.

Pulling her hair back and out of her face, Sophie picked up her phone, her keys, and her purse, and off she went. She sat in her car and turned it on, not quite sure where she'd end up. She wasn't sure if she'd end up at a new restaurant or anything else, but she had an idea: She had seen an idea for exploring the town on social media not too long. All she had to do was roll a dice a handful of times so she could figure out where she would go.

The rule of the game was that if she got a 1 or a 2 when she rolled, she would turn left at an intersection, if legal. If she rolled a 3 or 4, she would go straight, if legal, and if she rolled a 5 or 6, she would turn to the right. She was to do this for 10 different intersections, with three intersections passing any given direction before using the next roll. It was something that was supposed to be a fun date night idea for couples who are not really familiar with their area, but Sophie figured the universe would allow her to make an exception here—she didn't need anyone else to go with her at all.

So, she rolled the app on her phone six times, and she wrote down the following on her sticky note with her directions:

- *Left*
- *Straight*
- *Right*
- *Right*
- *Left*
- *Straight*

With that list in mind, it was time for her to explore. She turned on her car and began heading out from her home, thinking that every three intersections, she would follow the instructions given to her by the dice. Risky? Sure, but she thought it would be worth it.

Sophie quickly ducked into her car, covering up from the rain, and turned on the engine. Her sticky note of directions was stuck to the dash, and she was ready to go. She got to the exit of her subdivision, and the instructions began. She turned left and headed down the road. It was quietly forested where she was—she lived just north of the main part of town, barely outside of city limits. She drove down the road for a while, counting the intersections as they passed.

One... Two... Three... And then she had to turn left at the next intersection.

Sophie drove past a gas station, and a few bus stops shaded by trees as she drove down the dreary road. There were some dead-end streets that she passed that she chose not to count as intersections just due to the fact that she'd never get anywhere, and soon, she had crossed a little wooded creek. One... Two... And then there was a long stretch of road with nothing exiting off from it. It was nothing but trees all around, and while it was gorgeous, there would be no hiking through the mud for her. She finally made it to the third intersection, and her instructions sent her straight, so off she went.

This road found her on the ramp to get onto the freeway, and she shrugged. May as well see where it took her. She cruised along the freeway, counting the exits she passed. It eventually got to a place where there were four different split-offs, and a quick glance at her paper told her that she had to turn right, so she took the rightmost lane and found herself traveling south down the freeway. She passed the first three exits and then found herself taking a right turn off the road. A glance at her instructions told her she had to turn left and then go straight.

Following those instructions, she found herself on the southernmost outskirts of town—there wasn't very much out here but residential buildings and the occasional school or small building. It was cozy out there, and Sophie was actually quite unfamiliar with the area. She had never really had a reason to go through the area because she had never felt the need to. There really was nothing there if you didn't live there.

But, upon taking that final turn, she found herself in a parking lot. The parking lot led right into a cute little shopping strip. There was a small convenience store on one end, a post office in the center, and then a small local café on the other end. It was just the three buildings with maybe ten parking spots throughout the whole parking lot, and at the moment, four of them were filled up. She parked there and looked at the area that she had ended up in.

The café itself was called Coffee Maybe, and it was tucked underneath a big oak tree that was growing on the left, with a few small tables and chairs for people to enjoy their drink outdoors. Of course, this particular day did not lend itself to sitting outdoors, but it was nice that the option was there. She put her car in park and turned the engine off, then looked around. It was a nice enough area, that was for sure. The entire little strip of the building was impeccably maintained, nice and clean, and there was a cute little flower bed between the parking lot and the sidewalk leading up to the doors for each shop.

Sophie stepped outside, pulling her raincoat closer, and hustled all four steps to the entrance. She was ready to be away from the chilly rain, that was for sure. She walked right inside and dried her boots on the rug at the entry, and looked around.

The inside was surprisingly even cuter than outside. Along one wall, there were several coffee tables with reclining chairs, and on the left were walls of shelving, all filled up with board games and books for people to borrow if they chose to do so. The floor was a nice grey tile that was easily cleaned, and the entire place was dimly lit, but not in a bad way. It was very reminiscent of the time spent playing games in the late night at home at a sleepover as a kid, and she loved it. It looked like the perfect hangout place for the local high schoolers or college students, and though she was there alone, she felt herself wishing that she had brought some of her friends with her. Of course, she was there on her own, but that would be okay too. She was perfectly content to be there anyway. It was cozy.

The bar at the back of the café was immaculately kept. Shelves on the back wall were filled with just about every syrup type she could imagine. The whole place smelled of fresh coffee and pastries, and there was a big pastry case right in the front, with all sorts of sweet treats on display. In the back, she could hear the rumbling of a coffee machine as it brewed, and the whole place had quiet music, jazz it sounded like, playing to set the ambiance. The lights were pendant lights hanging down from the ceiling as well.

The cashier grinned and waved at Sophie as she looked around. "Thank you for coming to Coffee

Maybe, where coffee is always a yes! Can I help you?"
The cashier was a young girl, maybe 19, and she had
her long, auburn hair pulled into a ponytail. She wore
a plain black ¾ sleeved top and had an apron over it.

"Yeah, uh... Sorry, I've never been here before. Could I
have a sec, please?" Sophie replied sheepishly,
shoving her hands into her pockets as she stared up at
the menu. It looked pretty typical—divided by
mochas, cappuccinos, lattes, iced drinks, smoothies,
and even frappes. It was too cold for anything iced on
that rainy day, though, so she ignored the sweet treats
listed there and focused instead on the other items on
the list.

There were so many different combinations that
Sophie felt a bit overwhelmed, and with every passing
second, she felt a bit more anxious about how long it
was taking her to look over the menu. She hesitated a
moment before saying, "So, uh... What would you
recommend? What's your favorite?"

"Oh, that's easy! I'm so glad we have our pumpkin
spice flavors back in stock now that the season is
changing! My favorite is the pumpkin spice latte or
the pumpkin spice white chocolate mocha. It's
delicious!" The young girl was practically vibrating
with energy, and Sophie laughed a bit. She had clearly
had her fair share of that pumpkin spice that day.

"Sounds good. Let's do a medium pumpkin spice
white chocolate mocha." She had never tried
combining the two, but it sounded promising—after

all, there are pumpkin white chocolate cookies. Why not coffee?

"Great! Anything else? We have some delicious pumpkin pastries today, fresh from Bacrena Bakery down the street. They're freshly made and delivered still warm every morning, and oh man," she added, making the chef's kiss motion with her hands. "Delicious! You can't beat it, especially not with this weather. I can warm up one of the scones if you'd like?"

"Sure!" Sophie said with a quick smile back. She may as well—she was already there.

"Great! That'll be $9.42, please!" she cashier replied after punching the order into the computer.

Sophie passed her a debit card and looked around a bit more at the store. It was slow, surprisingly enough. There was an old man sitting at one table, looking out the window as he sipped at his coffee, just watching the rain and the occasional car drive by. It was a very sleepy area—not much traffic passed on foot or by car.

Upon receiving her card back, Sophie walked off, hesitating for a moment before approaching the lonely old man. "Excuse me," she said softly as she approached.

The old man didn't seem like he had expected to be talked to, and he looked up with mild curiosity. "Yes?"

he asked. He looked excited to be approached, and he smiled at her.

"Mind if I join you?" asked Sophie, gesturing to the empty seat. "It's been a long, boring day without anyone to talk to, and I could use the company." She smiled shyly.

"Of course, dearie, make yourself comfortable!" He scooted his drink and book over to make space on the other half of the table. "It's definitely one of those days, isn't it?"

"Yeah, it's the rain, I bet! It's so hard to feel like there's anything to do when it's so soggy outside. That's why I came here. My wife and I used to come here all the time when it rained." He smiled wistfully, his gaze far away as he reminisced for a moment. "Her favorite was to come here in the fall when the leaves changed colors, and she would order herself one of those fancy pumpkin lattes. She loved the spices, she always said, and she would sip away at them. I always went with plain drip coffee. But… She loved the sweetness." He looked down at his drink for a moment and took a sip. "Now that she's gone, I like to

come here from time to time as well to enjoy a drink
in her honor."

Sophie nodded her head in understanding. "I'm sorry
for your loss."

"Me, too," he replied, looking over at the barista, who
was walking over with Sophie's drinks.

"I've got a pumpkin spice white chocolate mocha and
pumpkin scone for Sophie," she said, placing them
down on the table in front of her.

"Sophie?" the old man asked incredulously.

"Mhm," she said as she brought the cup to her lips to
take the first sip of the fresh coffee, closing her eyes
and savoring it. It was surprisingly delicious, she
realized. The white chocolate added sweetness, but it
wasn't overwhelming. She smiled at him.

"My wife's name was Sophie," he said, his eyes tearing
up a bit. "Well, Sophie, it's very nice to meet you. I'm
Al."

"Nice to meet you, Al," she replied softly with a smile.
It sounded like she had ended up exactly where she
was meant to be. And, for the rest of the rainy
afternoon, she and Al spent the day chatting away as
they enjoyed each other's company.

Story 5: House Hunting

Cara is house hunting! She's touring a local mansion that she is interested in buying, and she's bringing Sophie along for the ride. Sophie gets to spend the day exploring an extravagant, 10,000 square foot property on the outskirts of town, and she wants to make sure that she's not all alone while she does it. Sophie is thrilled! She loves looking at properties, and this one will be plenty of fun.

"Are you ready, darling?" Cara purred as she peeked her head right into the front door of Sophie's home. She didn't knock—she never did, but Sophie didn't mind. Cara was like a sister to her, and she was thrilled to be included on such an important journey. But, she was running a bit behind, as usual. Bella woofed once in greeting before calmly trotting over to visit Cara as she popped inside, closing the door behind her. She petted the dog on the head and walked to sit at the dining table.

"Almost!" Sophie called back from upstairs. She was in her closet, getting her clothes for the day. They would be doing a lot of walking that day—Cara was there to pick Sophie up for a nice tour of a mansion nearby. The house was sitting on four acres of land, leading up to a strip of the Puget Sound, granting it instant beach access. From the pictures Sophie had seen, it was *gorgeous*. And she honestly hoped that her friend would buy it just because of the beauty of it. Cara was independently wealthy, having inherited her parents' multi-million dollar business that she had run for her, leaving her free to pursue her own interests in fashion. She was lucky, but she didn't let her wealth ruin her, either. Cara was very down to earth for someone who could literally afford to buy just about anything she wanted, and Sophie greatly respected her for it. Even now, with Cara sitting in her home, she knew that the entire downstairs level of the house was more or less the size of just one wing of that mansion they were heading out to look at, and she didn't mind one bit. Cara never gave her the impression that she thought that Sophie was incompetent or a failure. She never made Sophie feel like she was less than Cara due to money, either. In fact, Cara was actually incredibly generous more often than not, knowing that she was in a better financial position than most.

Within moments, Sophie was bounding down the stairs and to the main floor of her home. "Are you ready to go house hunting?" she asked with a big grin on her face.

"Am I!" Cara replied, flashing back a big smile as well. Cara was dressed impeccably in a nice baby blue pantsuit with a pair of flats that she slid onto her feet. The suit was clearly tailored to just her size, fitting just right on all the curves, and it looked great on her. Her blonde hair was neatly straightened, falling just past her shoulders, and she stood up from her seat at the table. "Let's get going!"

They hopped into Cara's car and were ready to go. The house wasn't too far away from where they were—maybe thirty minutes out of town, but it would be worth it. The day was sunny, and they would actually get to see the full beauty of everything in all its glory, and they were looking forward to it.

Before long, they had driven just out of town and had deviated off of the freeway to begin driving toward the Sound itself. The house was nestled against one of the dips inward, and as they pulled up to it, they were greeted with a wide expanse of forest. They were so far out that there was no way that they'd be seeing neighbors any time soon. The houses were on massive plots of land to grant that privacy, and they had been well planted to ensure that the privacy was maintained as well.

They pulled up to the parking spot, and both of them gasped in awe. They parked outside a garage entrance and saw that the walls of the house were beautiful white masonry, sculpted carefully, and kept clean. They were not even dusty or dirty, and they didn't even see a single spider web or anything. The roof was gently sloped, showing that the entire house was just one floor of expansive space in several different wings. The house's front was filled with arching windows that went up the entire expanse, ending maybe a foot from the room, and they were perfectly clear—no grime was present at all. Despite being outdoors, they were crystal clear, and they could see straight into what they assumed was a great room.

"You ready?" asked Cara.

"More than you know," Sophie replied, looping one arm into Cara's and off they went further into the room. They were incredibly excited to see everything within the entrance, and off they went. The ground underneath their feet was perfectly laid out concrete slabs with marble tiles shaping a path straight to the entrance. On either side of the entrance to the house, there were two perfectly cultivated gardens, complete with the most beautiful Japanese maple trees on either side, shielding over the entryway. It was a beautiful space, just walking up and inside was even better.

Right as they walked up, they saw the doors open, and a woman wearing a professional suit ushered them inside. "Welcome! Welcome!" she announced with a flourish of her arms. "It's nice to see you, Ms. Linn," she said, nodding to Cara with a smile. She clearly knew exactly who her customer was. "And you are?" she asked, turning her attention to Sophie.

"I'm Sophie Rogers," she replied with a smile and extended her hand. The realtor nodded and shook her hand.

"My name is Robin Evans," she replied curtly. She didn't seem nearly as interested in Sophie as in Cara, and Sophie couldn't really blame her. She wasn't the one about to put down money on a multi-million dollar property after all. She was the one that was just there for moral support and to see the beautiful architecture throughout the house.

As they stepped indoors, they were surrounded by tile. It was gorgeous indoors, and the floor was the most beautiful red cherry that Sophie had ever seen. The trim on the walls matched the floors throughout everything that they could see in the area. Even the furniture was that beautiful cherry color everywhere they went. It was impeccably matched from item to item and from room to room, and she couldn't believe just how beautiful it was going through it all. She was in awe of the beauty all around her.

The great hall was the first room that they went through. It had vaulted ceilings with massive skylights filtering in as much sunlight as possible, and there were couches lined up all around on the ground. The floor was that same beautiful cherry wood, and the couches were each immaculately white—as if they had never seen a speck of dust before. They were perfect— they looked so nice that Sophie felt herself wondering if they were walking through a staged showroom rather than an actual home that had been lived in before. She was shocked—there was no way that this was a home that someone else lived in. There was no way that a home that actually saw usage would be so impeccably neat.

But, then again, there was so much space open throughout the whole place that it was entirely possible that they just never used the same areas enough to ever actually make much of a difference to it. Sophie looked around slowly. The art on the walls was abstract—lots of colors that seemed to clash together, and she wasn't quite sure she knew what to make of it. She looked at it for a long while, eyes slowly skating over the whole thing. There was so much going on that she couldn't quite tell what was what, and she was unsure how that made her feel. But, one thing was true—she had to appreciate that the colors were nice and they matched well with everything else that was there.

There was a sitting area next to a grand fireplace, built into the wall with immaculate masonry out of granite with marble white pillars and mantle surrounding it. There was no fire burning at the moment, and Sophie wasn't really surprised—it was hot. She had to wonder, however—if they used it, did it get soot all over everything? Did it cause problems for the staff that probably cleaned up the room?

Before she could really wonder about it much longer, she found herself being tugged away by Cara as they moved on to the next room—the kitchen. The kitchen was the most exciting part of Sophie. While she wasn't much of a cook herself, she loved seeing the grand setups that people came up with on their own. She loved being able to see what people came up with and kitchens, being one of the most commonly used rooms in a house, always felt like a great place to start understanding the mind of someone else when you were in them. Sophie looked around as they walked in. The floor was black and white tiles, something that she never thought that she would appreciate, but upon taking that closer look, she realized that she loved it. They weren't actually that ugly when they were done intentionally. The counters were made of granite as well. The cabinetry, however, was the best part of what she was seeing. As she looked up, she realized that the cabinetry was designed carefully, intricately carved to display some beautiful flower-like designs that curled up the cabinets and all around the corners. They were immaculate, and they looked hand-done, which was even more impressive. Each cabinet was painted a fresh white color, and stainless steel appliances filled the room. There was a double oven in one counter setting, with a gas range with six burners quite close by. The fridge was massive, with French doors and a drawer underneath for the freezer. Overall, each appliance clearly was picked to match, shiny, and polished and without so much as a fingerprint marring the surface.

There was a big island bar in the center of the kitchen space, with barstools lining up on one side, and above it, there was a rack that was designed to hold all of the pots and pans up overhead. There was an assortment of gourmet pots and pans dangling there, waiting for action, but Sophie felt like they had never actually been used.

Again, Sophie felt Cara's touch, and when she turned to look, she saw her friend tilting her head, ushering her into the next room after they had undoubtedly finished discussing whatever it was that they were there to talk about. Off they went to the next room: A dining space that appeared designed to showcase a massive table that was almost certainly there to entertain people, judging by the number of chairs. There were at least eight on each side of the table, with two on each end as well, giving space for 20 people to sit and enjoy a meal.

The tabletop was granite, and there were massive pillars of the most beautiful cherry wood legs there to support the space. Each chair was a deep red leather, with brass legs, and they were all pushed into place carefully. On one end of the room, there was a massive cabinet that went up all the way to the ceiling, made of the same deep red wood that the rest of the house seemed so quick to showcase. In this room, the tile was a light, sandy color, giving some brightness to the space, and along the other wall, there was plenty of space and countertops for more food to be stored if necessary. The whole room was very well designed, and a big chandelier hung overhead, each crystal sparkling brightly and shining vividly.

They continued to go through room after room, but after a while, Sophie found herself getting restless. She wanted to find something else to do that would catch her attention longer. So far, she felt like every room was just more of the same, and after a while, she was simply bored. She didn't care to see three iterations of a kitchen in one house or so many rooms that she could hardly count them. Some of the rooms seemed just redundant—they would have similar setups in different colors or with different art up on the walls, and she found herself wondering what the point of so much space was in the first place.

But soon, they made it to the part of the tour that she found herself the most interested in seeing: The outdoors. They were heading toward the private beach that overlooked the Sound, and she was confident that it would be even more stunning in a real lie. As she walked out, they made their way to a beautiful porch overlooking the beach with a dock heading right out all the way into the water. It looked like a yacht could be parked there. The tile underfoot was smooth as well and looked almost wet—but it was simply the sheen that was on there. A hot tub sat underneath a large shade, and there was a nice outdoor dining set there as well. The view was unrivaled by anything else. It was gorgeous—the sun was starting to set by that point, and the sky was tinged a beautiful shade of magenta, with a sunburst orange color on the horizon as the sun fell behind the Sound.

"Wow," Sophie gasped as she looked out. "That view is *amazing*." She smiled as she looked over it, wishing that she would be able to get a view like that more often. It wasn't often that a view made her stop speaking in awe, but this one did. It didn't get much better than that view right there, and she felt like anything else that they saw after that point would be a waste of time—she felt like that would be the best possible end to their tour.

The realtor came up behind her. "Sure is something, isn't it?" she said wistfully as she looked at the sunset.

Sophie glanced over in surprise that she was being spoken to. "Yeah, it's gorgeous." She smiled. "I'm sure you get to see views like this all the time, huh?"

"Something like that," she replied, glancing to the ground and smiling for a moment. "But being able to see the houses, walk through it all, and just envision what life is like on the other side... it's amazing, isn't it? It's so *luxurious*."

Sophie nodded her head in response. It really was. She couldn't quite imagine leaving her life behind to live in what amounted to almost ten houses the size of her own. She thought it was beautiful, but she felt like she would get lost with all of those rooms out and about. She loved to look at everything, but she felt like ultimately, her own home was better suited for her and was perfectly designed for the space that she would need for herself. She didn't want to be totally overwhelmed—she wanted to be comfortable in her surroundings, and her house was exactly right.

"So, ready to go?" Cara called out from behind Sophie, making her turn her head. Cara looked exhausted but happy after the long day of trekking through all

10,000 square feet of house and so much of the acreage outside.

Sophie nodded. "Thanks for your time," she told the realtor, who smiled and waved in return.

"You two take care. And Cara, dear, you know how to reach me if you need anything!"

Cara waved back as they left.

As they sat down in the car, Cara let out a big sigh and flopped against the back seat. "Man, that house was *big*."

"Yeah, it was!" Sophie chimed back. "What do you think about it?"

"I think I'd be too tired to walk around so much! It's much too big for me!" Cara wiped her brow off and closed her eyes. "I might stick to closer to the city—at least I can walk across your house without getting winded."

Sophie laughed. "That is true!" she said as Cara started up the car to head home. It turned out, even Cara thought that there was such thing as too much house, and that one was it.

Story 6: Missed Connections

On a cool autumn day, Sophie went out for lunch at a local bistro, only to find that her old college roommate was also there enjoying a meal! Together, they sat down and had a nice, long chat to catch up with each other and see what was up with each other's lives.

Sophie closed up her laptop with a sigh to herself. Her stomach was rumbling, and even though she knew that she had more work to get through, she knew that work would be infinitely harder if she didn't take the time to eat. She needed to find a way to eat something to keep her energy up and keep her mind focused on the work that she needed to do. With a stretch of her arms, she glanced at the clock. It was lunchtime, for sure.

Standing up, she walked into her kitchen, opening up the fridge. It was shockingly empty—all that was in there was a half-gallon of milk, a small container of yogurt, some butter, peanut butter, and ketchup. It was a strange hodgepodge of ingredients, and she sighed. "Guess I shouldn't have skipped grocery shopping..." she told herself with a sigh as she closed the fridge door. It was pretty typical for her to run out of food—she was only one person, and she didn't eat nearly as much as many other people seemed to. Of course, not buying that food often led to her also having to deal with the consequences—primarily needing to order out. Of course, ordering out also usually cost more money that she would have to spend, but that was okay—at least she would have delicious food to enjoy without having to cook and without having to clean up the mess afterward. Win, win!

But, that also meant that she had to find something new to eat, too, and that was always the hardest part of it all. How did she choose out what to enjoy when there were so many different options? How could she choose out what her meal would be when there were nearly limitless choices around her? Just within a five-minute radius, she had a teriyaki restaurant, a ramen restaurant, a sushi restaurant, an authentic Mexican restaurant, a Chinese restaurant, an Indian restaurant, two Thai restaurants, a few burger joints, and just about every fast-food chain imaginable. There were so many options, and if she were to get just a bit further away from home, she would have even more options to enjoy as well.

With a sigh, she scrolled through a list of local restaurants on her phone. She looked over the, one at a time, and tried to figure out what the right one was for her. She wasn't totally confident in the choices— but then she realized that there was one name on the list that she hadn't recognized: Sunnyside Bistro. It was just five minutes away, and she remembered that it had been opened maybe a week prior. It was supposed to be locally sourced ingredients that would create delicious dishes. It was open for brunch, lunch, and dinner daily, and she had heard that it was supposed to be great. It was opened up by the owners of another restaurant that was delicious and did well in the area.

Well, it was always good to try new things, she told herself as she looked around. And this was the perfect opportunity to do so. After all, many of the blogs that she wrote on a regular basis would encourage people to try new things to enjoy life, and why not? Trying new things brought variety, and variety was supposed to be the spice of life, right? It sounded perfect and like a nice way to break up the monotony of her day.

After quickly getting ready to go and put on an oversized beige sweater to go with her skinny jeans and boots, she grabbed her purse and rushed out the door, keys, and phone in hand. The bistro was really just a few blocks away, and if it hadn't been so chilly, she would have considered just walking. But, given the volatility of the weather, she figured better safe than sorry. She didn't really want to get wet.

Within minutes, she was there, pulling her car into park and getting herself situated. She was ready to enjoy her lunch. She had spent the whole three-minute drive, thinking all about what she was going to eat and how enjoyable it all was going to be. Sophie's stomach gurgled and growled again, and she rubbed it absently for a moment as she pulled out the keys and stepped out of her car. Lunch was calling.

As she stepped into the little bistro, she noticed that it was mostly empty. There was only one other person there, sitting in a corner, head down and in a book.

The waitress working, upon seeing Sophie, waved and ushered for her to follow. "Right over here, please!" she said kindly with a smile. Sophie followed readily as the waitress gathered up a menu and a bundle of silverware, setting it down in the table across from the one that the other person was sitting at.

As Sophie got settled, the waitress ran off to get her a glass of water, and she flipped through the menu. It had all the usual choices one would expect in a bistro. There were a maybe a dozen different choices plus a make-your-own-panini section listed as she skimmed through it. There were so many different options there for her to choose from—she just needed to figure out which one sounded the best.

The waitress came back with a fresh glass of cold water. "Do you need another minute to glance over the menu?" she asked with a smile.

"Mmm.... No, I think I'm good," Sophie replied with a smile.

"Oh, great! And what can I get for you today?"

"I'll take the turkey basil Panini, please."

"Great choice!" the waitress informed her, nodding her head sagely as she wrote down the order. "That's one of our most popular sandwiches, and it's delicious! Anything else for you?"

"Nope, that'll do it. Thanks!" Sophie passed the menu back over to the waitress and took a sip from her water, pulling her phone out to mindlessly scroll through social media. It wasn't like she had much better to do at the moment—she just had to wait for her dish to be brought out for her.

"Sophie Rogers is that you?"

Just as Sophie was about to read through her next image collection, she heard someone call her name behind her. Turning around, she was greeted by a young woman about her age, with pixie-short brunette hair, pale skin, and petite features. Her big, blue eyes looked at Sophie incredulously. But, it was the perfect little mole on the right cheekbone that jogged Sophie's memory.

"Wow, Sylvia, is that you?" She smiled at the woman sitting at the table. "Ohmigosh, it's been so long!!"

"I know! What have you been up to? You look great!" Sylvia replied, grinning from ear to ear. Sylvia always had that air about her—she was someone that was wrapped up in all levels of positivity, and her excitement was always contagious.

"Not much! I'm just writing articles these days. I've got an adorable German shepherd named Bella, but other than that, it's just me! How about you?" Sophie was glad—Sylvia looked like she was genuinely doing well. She looked healthy, comfortable, and even better, just as happy as she used to be. Her happiness practically emanated off of her, and Sophie was so relieved to see it. She always loved seeing people that she used to know doing well—it gave her hope.

"Come over here!!" Sylvia said, gesturing for her to come to the table with her, and Sophie obliged, hopping over to the other chair. She took her water with her and smiled, settling down and resting her chin on her hands with her elbows propped onto the surface. "So then, a dog, huh? No kids? No special someone?"

"Nope, just my dog!" Sophie smiled at her friend. "What about you?" She was more interested to hear about Sylvia than to talk about herself. After all, they had lost touch long, long ago. The two of them had shared a dorm together when they were freshmen in college. They had been quite different from each other, but they got along well. Sylvia was down to earth—she had studied mathematics with the goal of being a math teacher for middle school. She had always been someone that wanted to help reach out to those who needed it the most, and she loved the idea of getting through to stubborn children, teaching them to love something that they initially rejected. "Are you a teacher yet?"

Sylvia smiled and shook her head. "Nope! That line didn't really work out."

"Oh?" Sophie was curious—the Sylvia she knew was so passionately driven toward that degree path. She was so determined to be that teacher. It was actually mildly shocking to Sophie that she wasn't interested in the least. However, Sophie also knew that it wasn't really her business, and though it was surprising, if Sylvia had found something else to occupy her time, then that was great, too. After all, Sylvia had that sort of happy glow to her—Sophie couldn't quite put her finger on where it was coming from, but it looked good on her.

"Actually, I'm married now," she said, holding up a hand to reveal a wedding ring wrapped delicately around her ring finger. It was a beautiful rose gold ring that complemented her skin perfectly, and there was one diamond—not too big or too small—sitting right at the front of it.

Sophie gasped, pulling her hands up to cover her mouth while her eyes widened. "No way!!" She squealed, barely able to contain her excitement for her friend. "Congratulations!! So who's the lucky guy?"

"Do you remember Drake? The chemistry major?"

"Dorky Drake? The really shy one that always tried to avoid confrontations, even when he really shouldn't be?" asked Sophie, trying to remember.

"That's the one! He's not so dorky anymore, though." Sylvia smiled fondly as she pulled out her phone, unlocking the screen and turning it around to show Sophie. The picture had Drake, the same man she had remembered. But, he looked more mature. His skin had cleared up from the acne that it had been covered in before, and he looked like he was genuinely happy. He wore a confident smile, and his hair was slicked back. He was dressed in a nice pair of slacks with a white button-down shirt and polished shoes, and hanging to his arms was Sylvie, standing just barely at his shoulder height. She was looking up at him with an affectionate smile.

But, what stood out the most to Sophie was Sylvia's stomach.

It was round.

"Do you have a baby?" Sophie blurted out unceremoniously, eyes getting even wider as she looked at her friend.

"Not yet!" Sylvia said with a smile, pushing her seat back. Sophie hadn't realized it, but her old friend's belly was swollen with a baby. She looked about ready to pop at any moment!

"Wow!" Sophie breathed out. "You look so good!" It was true—Sylvia was carrying that pregnancy like a natural, and Sophie realized that was what was giving her that joyful, youthful glow to her—it was the pregnancy glow. "Is it a boy or a girl?"

"Both!"

"Both?"

"Twins! One boy, one girl." Sylvia rubbed her belly affectionately. "We've got another four weeks to go before these two are done baking. Hopefully, it goes by quickly! I don't know if I could carry them for much longer at this rate!" She laughed. "I'm kinda starting to feel like I'm in beached whale form."

"No!" Sophie gasped. "You look fantastic! And besides, not everyone can carry a twin pregnancy. I'd say you're doing absolutely wonderfully." She nodded her head resolutely. So many pregnant women would put far too much pressure on themselves to look good, and it drove Sophie insane. There was no reason for her to feel so harshly about herself. "But, do you have any names chosen out?"

"We do!" Sylvia replied. "We're naming the little girl Luna Vivian, and the boy is going to be named Damon James."

"What stunning names!" Sophie replied after a moment to mull over the names. They flowed well off of the tongue, and both names were gorgeous. She loved them and could only hope that when it was her turn to name her own children, she could have as good of taste.

"Thanks!" Sylvia replied, taking a sip of her water as she smiled. She got a faraway look in her eyes before rubbing her belly again. "They're definitely going to be a handful," she mused.

"Oh, man, I bet. But you'll manage! So, are you staying home with them?" Sophie was definitely curious about her old friend's plans. She had always been the type to say that she had no interest in

"That's the plan! It'll be the three of us while Drake heads out to work every day."

Sophie nodded her head. "Makes sense! Man, the daycare costs… That sounds awful." She took another sip of water as she looked at her old friend. It was crazy to see just how far her peers ended up in life. It was interesting just how many different directions everyone would go down. Some would make the shift toward domestic life or having families, as Sylvia was doing. It was great to see them settling down happily, enjoying where they were with their relationships. Others were full steam ahead in their careers.

"I know! Plus diapers for two? It's crazy. But it'll be worth it!"

"I'm sure," replied Sophie. It certainly sounded like it would be. So many women felt that pull toward having children—they were driven by their desire to mother others. Sophie, however, wasn't sure she felt that pull. She didn't know whether what she wanted was to have her own children or to be her own person. It was hard to know where to fall between the two when she didn't feel a pull one way or the other. She wasn't quite sure where she wanted to be in life. She had her dog, and she had her home, and for the moment, that was enough. For the moment, she was perfectly satisfied with where she was, and she would have plenty of time to find her way later on.

Both Sophie and Sylvia fell silent for the moment. They both sat there quietly. It was slightly awkward and uncomfortable—the kind of silence that lingers just a bit too long with people who have grown distant. Sophie's gaze slipped away, looking out the window at the dreary sky as she spaced out, just watching the cars drive by, and Sylvia glanced down at her cup of water.

"Well," Sophie said finally, breaking the silence, "I'm glad that you are doing so well. It's really refreshing to see people living their best lives." She smiled genuinely at her friend. She really meant well for her dear old friend.

"It's nice to see you doing so well, too! We'll have to catch up again more often. Do you live here?" Sylvia asked.

"Yes, I'm maybe five minutes from here. Just figured I'd try a new restaurant today!"

"Wow! I'm maybe five minutes away too. We'll have to meet up more often. You'll have to come and visit when the babies come! I'm sure Drake would enjoy seeing you again, too. It's always nice to catch up with people after a while!" Sylvia picked up her purse. "But, I've actually gotta run—Got an OB appointment in a few! It was so nice to see you here again, Sophie!"

Sophie nodded in agreement. Meeting up again sounded great, and she was totally down to do so again. She scribbled her phone number down on a piece of paper from her own purse and passed it over to Sylvia. "Just send me a quick text when you're feeling up to another meeting!"

"Will do! See you later!" And with that said, Sylvia headed out the door and off to her appointment.

Sophie gathered her items up and turned back to her own seat, where she had been. She sipped at her water and went right back to scrolling through her phone. Just as she did, a message popped up:

"Nice to see you again!
XO
Sylvia"

Sophie smiled to herself. How nice! And, just as she read the message, the waitress came back with her sandwich. The panini was perfectly grilled, with a nice, generous helping of fries next to it. It looked great! "Thank you!" she told the waitress as the food was put right in front of her.

"Enjoy!" replied the waitress as she left Sophie to her own devices.

Sophie didn't need to be told twice—she was thrilled to have her food. Her stomach gurgled again as she took a big bite. It was perfect. The sandwich was cooked perfectly, and the taste was better than she could have imagined.

Of course, that could also have just been the hunger that she was feeling, too. She was *famished*.

Story 7: Variety Is the Spice of Life

After a few days of boring deadlines that had to be met, Sophie is ready for some real change! She is determined to make a difference in her day, and she has decided that she will do that by trying to do something new. Her new thing of the day is shadowing strangers in the park.

"I'm so bored," Sophie moaned to herself as she threw herself onto her bed. She was tired of not having anything to do and was more than ready to find something exciting. She needs variety! She needed thrill! She needed *excitement!* Anything would do, so long as it broke the monotony of the day. She just had to find something. *Anything.*

Sighing, she stared up at the white, textured ceiling that she had meant to paint. She had been thinking about it for ages, but she had never bothered painting her master bedroom. White was good enough for her as far as she cared—at least it was painted. But, she knew that she'd have to get to it eventually. The task went onto her to-do list that she constantly had growing on the backburner. It would get done eventually, she told herself offhandedly as she looked around her room.

She pulled her phone over to herself and started scrolling through her usual sites. Maybe she'd find something interesting to do somewhere online; she thought as she looked through everything listlessly. She wasn't exactly having much fun as she went through everything. But then, she saw it: The thing that she would do to cure her boredom.

On a page of random ways to pass the time, she stumbled upon the shadowing game. The idea of the game was that she had to follow around someone in public for as long as possible until they noticed that she was. The longer that she could get with following them around, the better. It sounded fun! Vaguely creepy, she had to admit, but also like harmless fun. She wasn't going to be bothering anyone—she'd just be following them around for as long as possible to see what would happen. She figured that she might as well give it a shot—after all, she had nothing else to do.

So, Sophie set out to have a little bit of fun. She was determined to enjoy herself somehow, and a bit of a thrill was definitely in order. After getting dressed, putting on a white long sleeve shirt with horizontal stripes, a pair of skinny blue jeans, taupe booties, and a military green faded canvas jacket, she was ready to go. The best place she figured she could go to have some fun would be in the mall—there were always plenty of people wandering about, and she figured that she would have luck finding someone to follow there. With her purse over her shoulder and her determination steeled, she set off.

The mall was only ten minutes away from home for Sophie, and it was surprisingly empty. Or, maybe it wasn't surprising considering that it was early afternoon on a Wednesday. People were at work—it was normal working hours. But, Sophie wasn't willing to let that cause her any problems—she was determined to enjoy her day! She parked her car in the parking lot and figured she'd take the time to enjoy the moment. She set off, striding with purpose and determination that, as she got closer and closer to the mall's entrance.

As she got closer and closer, it felt more and more real, and she realized that she was about to start her game. She faltered for a moment. Was she being weird? She felt like she kind of was. But, that voice in the back of her mind pushed her forward. It told her that she had to at least try—may as well. She drove out all that way, and the least that she could do was make it a point to actually do something while there.

So, she went off and started looking around the mall. She needed to find someone that wouldn't be mean about things. It had to be someone who would be likely to laugh off what she was doing. Maybe someone looked like they weren't a very serious person. It would have to be someone that looked like they were going to be friendly, and someone who wouldn't be worried that she was trying to rob them.

Sophie looked around, trying to find a good option. There weren't many. She saw a woman walking with young children, but in her experience, they were usually the most likely to be offended or bothered by someone following them because they would be afraid that they were genuinely going to be hurt.

Sophie felt a pang of guilt at the thought—she just wanted to have some fun trying something new. This seemed like something spunky and spontaneous, and that meant that it had to be a good option, right?

She wasn't so sure at that point—she was starting to doubt that she had made the right choice at all. After all, these were just unsuspecting people out at the mall, looking to enjoy their day. With a sigh, Sophie plopped herself down on the nearest bench and looked at the people that passed by.

There was a mother toting two children along with her, both of which looked miserable. The boy was maybe 4, and he was pouting and whining about something that Sophie couldn't quite make out, but judging by the parent's reaction, was something annoying or something that had been argued several other times in the past, and she was having none of that nonsense. The daughter was in a stroller, grumpily rubbing her eyes. The mother was the walking definition of a mombie. Her hair looked frizzy, and she looked like she was in dire need of a coffee. At that moment, Sophie did not envy that woman, nor did she really feel the urge to follow along and see what would happen next. After all, that seemed like it was just asking for trouble.

The next person to go by was actually a group of people—they were 20-something men walking through the mall with a couple of bags from the local sports shop. They were laughing together about some sort of inside joke, judging by the exaggerated eyebrow waggling and the tilts of the head. Sophie sighed. They wouldn't have been much fun to follow either and, in fact, would seem like the kind of people that would do nothing but cause her problems. So, they were crossed off the list, too. Nope, no, thank you, Sophie told herself.

The third person she saw pass was a man all by himself. He was staring down at his phone as he walked by, with a serious expression on his face, and he looked like he really needed to get something off his chest, but he wasn't sure how to do so. He looked around at the surroundings with a sigh, wondering what he was going to do next, and Sophie quirked a brow. She kind of wanted to see what he was going to do.

Before she knew it, she stood up and started to follow him from a distance. He was walking down a major strip of the mall slowly, almost leisurely. His gaze drifted lazily from store to store as he tried to make out what he was looking for. Sophie wondered briefly what he was looking for, and she had to bite her tongue to keep herself from asking him. She didn't want to out herself; after all—she needed to make sure that he didn't catch that she was behind him. She would have to be very careful to make sure that she was unnoticed. If she could do her job the right way, she would be able to get through the whole mall and figure out whatever it was that he was looking for.

He stopped first at a store that looked like it was meant to sell trinkets in general. There were many little blown glass figurines hanging out in the front, and they sparkled in the fluorescent lighting of the mall. Sophie could admire them from her spot a few feet back. They were shimmering in the light, and in particular, Sophie found herself staring in awe at an owl that was suspended in the air, its crystalline wings sparkling as they refracted light and glimmers of sparkles all over the surrounding surfaces. The owl was gracefully swooping, wings spread, and eyes fixed on something as it did, and Sophie couldn't take her eyes off of it. It looked so great that she had to keep on staring. In fact, she stared so long at that adorable little figurine that she realized she completely lost where he was in the first place. She lost track of the man that she had been trailing. Inwardly kicking herself, she scoped out the area.

He was wearing a black collared shirt and slim-cut slacks that hugged his frame nicely, highlighting just how in shape he was. His sandy hair was cut relatively short, with a small flair of hair in the front that was slicked back. She knew that he couldn't have gone too far, and she looked around for black clothes.

But, she realized at that moment that black seemed to be as trendy as ever—there were a lot of teens and men wearing black shirts and black pants that appeared to be slim cut. And, he had been an average height in general—it wasn't exactly easy to find this man with is virtually basic look. With a sigh, Sophie shook her head. She had definitely lost that one.

"Excuse me, ma'am, you look lost," a deep voice purred from behind her, almost tantalizingly teasing as it spoke.

Sophie turned around in curiosity, only to find herself face to face with none other than the man that she had been following. He was smirking at her, almost playfully, as she watched him in embarrassment and horror. Her cheeks burned as they turned bright pink, and her eyes widened as she stumbled and tripped over the worlds that she had to say. How could she possibly explain the game that she was playing and how harmless it was when she had just been following someone around? How could she possibly spin this, so she didn't sound like she was absolutely crazy? It was difficult at best—especially because she *was* following him around.

He quirked a brow at her lack of a response, his smirk growing more satisfied as she grew more flustered. With a huff, Sophie crossed her arms. "Can I help you?" she asked him.

"I believe I should be asking you that question, not the other way around," he bantered back. He had a point, too. "Why were you following me? If you wanted my number, you could have just asked." He winked at her playfully. He was clearly enjoying every minute of her suffering, and he was dragging it out as much as he could, too.

Sophie huffed again and averted her gaze, arms crossing defensively in front of her chest. "It's nothing, really. It's a silly dare." She was really beginning to feel embarrassed the more that she spoke, and she had no idea how she was going to make it better. Ultimately, the best thing that she could think of to do was to tell him the truth.

"You see... I was actually just playing a game. I wanted to know how long I could follow someone before they noticed that I was. I saw it online, and I know that it was stupid, but I was bored and felt like it would help me to pass the time. I'm sorry for bothering you." The words tumbled out of her mouth before she could do a thing to sort of censor them, and she found herself staring at the ground, wishing that she could get it to open up from underneath her and eat her up. She really just wanted to disappear in the moment, but she had no clear escape.

"I see," said the man thoughtfully as he looked her over, head to toe. He seemed to be considering something, and Sophie hoped that he wasn't going to get her banned from the mall or something for harassing patrons. She loved the mall—she had just been bored and needed something to pass the time.

"I am really sorry," Sophie repeated again with a sigh.

"I don't believe I got your name," he replied almost coolly. Sophie was going crazy—she couldn't quite make out what he was thinking, and that made him next to impossible to read. His inscrutable gaze bore into her, leaving her squirming in her place. She was incredibly uncomfortable in the moment but could not think of a good way to break free. She felt stuck—after all, she owed him an explanation.

"Sophie," she replied shyly. She was shocked at the shyness—but she couldn't quite make it go away. She was *embarrassed*. She sighed to herself, running a hand through her hair. "Look, I'm sorry," she said, averting her gaze.

Sophie was expecting him to get mad or to yell or to tell her that she's a creep. But none of that happened. A long silence hung in the air for a few heartbeats, and then Sophie was surprised at what she heard: Laughter. She heard laughter.

The man was *laughing* at her.

Sophie looked up in shock, meeting his gaze. He seemed genuinely amused, and Sophie wasn't sure if she should feel relieved or disappointed as a result. She looked back down at her feet in embarrassment, unsure what to do next. But, then he spoke.

"Well, you were not very good at it." He quirked a brow at her and smiled. "You really have to work on that sneaking of yours. You were way too obvious, just slowly following me around. You didn't even look away! You were just staring right at me."

Sophie felt another, fresher wave of shame fill her. He had a point—she wasn't really careful at all. And, it backfired on her. She really was bad at this whole thing, and that was definitely something that she would have to deal with. But, more specifically, she knew that she would not be going out of her way to follow people again. Lesson learned. Experiment failed. She was entirely done with that line of thinking and action. It was time for her to go back to her boring life, doing boring things, and enjoying boring days. Variety might have been the spice of life, but really, Sophie had to admit that boringness was at least predictable. At least she knew what to expect, when to expect it. And, it wasn't as embarrassing.

"But, you know what? You'll have to learn from a pro next time. I like to make it a bit more obvious: I walk around and do something conspicuous just to see how long it takes for someone to realize that I'm following them. Sometimes I whistle a certain song the whole time. Other times, I will skip or ride a unicycle around. And even better—when they look at me all confused and wondering why I'm following them? I look around like they are, looking as confused as I can to see what happens."

Sophie was shocked. She hadn't expected him to be interested in some silly game like that—but she was a bit relieved that he seemed to think that it was actually funny. At least she didn't have him threatening to call the police or do something else that would have added a whole new layer of complications to the day.

"I'm Eric," he told her, holding out a hand to shake.

Sophie looked down at his hand and composed herself for a moment before taking it. "Nice to meet you," she said. She still felt embarrassed, but she was glad that things weren't a total problem for her. She was glad that he seemed like he was a lighthearted kind of person. He seemed friendly enough as well.

"So, bored, huh?" asked Eric. "That's something that can be fixed easier than stalking someone else through a mall, you know," he teased, once again smirking. He seemed amused by her internal squirming and her total embarrassment, and Sophie had to force her to take a deep breath and sigh.

"You're right. Next time maybe I'll just make it a point to just stroll right up and start a conversation!" Sophie told him with a smile.

"That's a wonderful idea, Sophie. We could have had a great, easy conversation that would have been a whole lot of fun. But now, you'll never know, will you? You really missed out, you know." Eric was watching her with a teasing expression.

"That's too bad, isn't it!" Sophie shrugged. "Well, Eric, I'll keep your suggestion in mind for the next time. I'll make sure that next time, I'll just walk right up to you.

But, for now, I gotta get going. I've got things to buy and people to see."

"You mean that owl you were watching?"

Sophie was shocked—he had been paying enough attention that he had noticed her. Wow, she was worse at this than she had thought for sure. Not only did she fail to stay out of sight, but she was also so bad at this that Eric was able to see exactly what she was doing. "Yeah," she said with an embarrassed smile.

"Well, Sophie, you're in luck." Eric held out a paper bag to her. It was a nice, lavender-colored bag with white handles, and the name of the store that she had passed was scrawled out across the top.

Sophie's eyes widened, and she looked down at the bag. "What's this?"

"Open it and find out," Eric replied with a wink.

Sophie opened it up, and inside was a box. Inside the box was that crystalline owl that she had been eyeing. It was perfect—the wings were shimmering, and she *loved* it. Her eyes widened up as she looked at it, and she looked up to Eric. "What, no!" She shook her head. "I can't accept this!"

"Please?" asked Eric. He smiled at her. "Consider it payment for the awkwardness." He refused to take the bag out of her hands as she offered it back.

Sophie sighed. "Okay," she said. "If you insist. Well…
Thank you." She smiled at him and looked down at
the gift.

"Just promise me that you'll make it a point to talk to
me the next time you see me instead of trying to
shadow me, okay?"

"Will do!" Sophie nodded her head. She smiled.

"Well, Sophie, I'm heading out. I'll see you later,
okay?" Eric smiled and waved at her as he turned
around. "Enjoy the day!" She smiled

"You, too!" Sophie slid the owl back into the bag and
turned around to leave her car. She smiled to herself
as she walked away. While things didn't quite work
out the way that she thought they would, she had met
someone new that seemed nice in his own way. She
was glad that she had the chance to talk to someone
else. So, off she went, heading back home. She
considered her lesson learned. No more crazy
suggestions from the internet when she needed
something to do for the day!

Guided Meditation 1: The Plateau of Inner Peace

Close your eyes and take in a big, deep breath. Feel the air flowing through your nose. Notice how it feels. Focus on the temperature and the smells. Feel it filling up your lungs, with your lungs swelling up within you like great, big balloons in your chest until you feel like they can't swell up anymore. Feel the air warming in your chest and exhale slowly, feeling the air pass your lips gently and slowly. Is it warm? With each breath that you take, you feel yourself calming down.

You breathe in... And out...

Now, feel yourself. Focus on your center, the point just above your belly button. How does it feel? Is it tense? Tight? Stressed? Focus on this point as you inhale in. One... Two... Three... Four... Five... and out... One... Two... three... Four... Five... Focus on that spot for another breath or two...

Now, feel the tension in your body. Become aware of any tension you are holding in your head and face. As you breathe in, imagine that you are pushing the tension down to the center above your belly button. Let it gather there. Now, feel the tension in your shoulders. Focus on that stress and tension and as you breathe in, feel it moving down to your center. Let it gather there, imagining your tension and stress all becoming balled up in the center. Feel the tension in your arms and hands gathering and flowing into your center. Feel that center growing with the tension and allow it to build up. Then, take the tension from your chest and upper back, and flow it down toward your center.

Then, go down to your toes and feet, identifying the tension that is there. Push it up, feeling it flowing up your legs, through your pelvis and belly, and noting it as it arrives in the belly. Focus on it as it grows within you and allow it to flow.

Feel all of the tension in your body, all boiled up into one big ball in your core. Allow yourself to feel the weight of that tension and the burden that it has been putting on you. Take in a deep breath as you focus on it. Then, bid it goodbye and goodnight.

As you exhale, pull the tension out from your core. Envision yourself picking up the ball of stress and tension and holding it like a basketball. Feel its heft in your mind. Inhale again. One... Two... Three... Four... Five... And as you exhale, throw the ball away from you. Watch as the ball of tension flies into the air. Watch it as it continues further and further away, getting smaller and smaller into the distance as you breathe. It is much smaller now, and soon, it is so small that you can no longer see it, and then it is completely gone.

Now, in that space where you pulled the tension away, in your center, imagine that peace and calmness flow into you. It is slowly manifesting within your core, filling you with peace, comfort, and the feeling that everything will be okay. You have a big, shining golden ball of peace and relaxation within your core. Breathe in... One... Two... Three... Four... Five... And out... One... Two... Three... Four... Five... As you breathe in, imagine the feeling of relaxation extending throughout your body. Feel it in your head. Breathe in... and out... Feel the relaxation pulsating in your shoulders and arms... Feel it spreading throughout your chest. Feel it spread down to your legs and feet. It fills your whole body, bringing you utter peace and relaxation. Your mind feels incredibly open and ready to go on a peaceful, relaxing adventure. Your body is ready to fall deeper and deeper into your relaxation so you can become more and more relaxed.

As you breathe, you fade away until you are surrounded by nothing but darkness. The darkness is friendly and calm, and you feel utterly relaxed as you bask in it. It is inviting and familiar. You feel it calling to you, reminding you that you are always at home when you come to this place. This place is your imagination; it is your innermost part of your mind and is a place where you control everything. It is a place that you can visit whenever you are finding yourself feeling stressed or unable to relax. Here, you can be at true peace with yourself. It is a place of potential and possibilities. It is a place where you are the master. You are the creator.

Out of the darkness, you see a point of light on the distance. It starts out small, one tiny point of light. With every breath you take, it gets longer. It starts to get a little bit bigger. The light is golden and warm, and it spreads out. Its rays begin to radiate through the darkness above you, and you start to realize that the darkness above you is transforming. It becomes filled with radiant hues of reds, oranges, and pinks, as the light in the distance gets larger and larger. It is a great, big orb, rising up into the sky and illuminating everything around you. The sun is rising in your imagination, lightening up your surroundings. The sun is your inner peace and relaxation that you have summoned within yourself. With every breath you take, it pulsates stronger and larger as it slowly creeps across the sky.

As the light spreads across your inner world, you feel yourself at peace. Your innermost environment is being illuminated with the relaxation. It is warming your body, and as it continues to glow, you feel yourself basking in the warm, early light. You feel calm, and the sky above you has erupted, painted with streaks of pink chasing away the darkness in the dawn. You take in another breath, feeling that all is right within your world. In your heart, you know that you are safe. You are calm. You are relaxed. You are ready to explore this inner world within yourself that you never knew existed.

You realize that you can move around in this space within yourself. You become aware that underneath you, there is a surface that you can walk upon. You can feel it, sturdy and supporting your body, underneath your feet, and you can feel the faint tickling of fresh, dew-kissed grass against your skin. It feels cold for a moment, but then it leaves you feeling refreshed. You look down, and you can see the softest, most verdant grass you have ever seen. It spreads around underneath your feet and all around you as well. If you will it, you can move about the world as well. You can walk. You can turn. You can move. This whole world exists within you, granting you that power over yourself that you can use to embrace the world. Reach out and take it,

You take one step effortlessly. Even if your body has pain, in your imagination, within yourself, it is painless to move. Your legs are strong, and they can carry you. They are powerful and supporting you. Your body is there to help you. It is there to be there for you. It loves you as only you can love yourself. As you move throughout your body, you realize that you are at peace within yourself.

As you take a step, you see that there are flowers growing behind you. With every step that you take, flowers spring up in your wake. You can see that there are marigolds, beautiful and red there as you walk. You can see irises, blue and tall. There are tiny pinkish bells of heather and bushy bunches of pansies growing all around you. Each step you take brings more into the world to dance about. Each step brings more beauty into the world.

Your own steps in the real world bring beauty as well. As you walk throughout the real world, you leave a trail in your wake. Your existence, your actions, and your presence will influence those around you. You leave your own mark on every single person that you meet, but in here, within yourself, you can physically sculpt the land. You can see the flowers, and you can smell their soft, sweet scents starting to waft up, a beautiful, bright fragrance that reminds you of a time when you were able to be in perfect peace with the world. You can feel your own peace and harmony with the world and with everyone around you. You can feel your own ability to relate to everyone around you. You can feel that you are perfectly at peace in your moment.

Now, you take a step as if you are walking up a stairway, and as you do so, you manifest a step out of nowhere. The step is almost cobbled in appearance, made of perfectly smooth stones that are warm beneath your bare feet. The step is almost perfectly molded to your feet, and you can feel yourself in the moment walking up them. Around the edges of the steps, you can see more of the flowers—snapdragons with bright orange heads this time. They sway in a breeze that tousles your hair but leaves you invigorated and calm. You feel confident. You feel at peace. You feel ready to keep exploring.

You take in a deep breath, soaking in the scent of the flowers, and you step once more, knowing that you cannot let yourself down. You step, knowing that your mind will not let you fall, and you are not disappointed. Another step, just as curiously cobbled as the last appears, just a little bit higher up this time. You take the step and see more snapdragons spring up all around it. You look around yourself, and you see the world beneath you. You can see your entire world—everything that you are—sprawling endlessly underneath the sun in the sky above you.

You continue your way up the stairs, going higher and higher, not knowing what to expect. As you walk up the stairs, you get further and further from the ground, but you do not feel afraid. You know that you are safe as you continue to walk your way up the stairs. You feel totally confident that you are in control and safe as you continue your way up them. You know that you can get there if you just keep going a little bit further... You are not sure where you are going yet, but in your heart, you know that the steps are taking you in the right direction. The more you go, the more confident that you are in the right direction. You look around yourself, and you can see nothing. You have climbed so high that the ground beneath you is nothing but a big, green patch, and above you, all you can see is the warm, early dawn sky. The colors are beautiful as they paint the clouds above you, refracting the pinks and oranges as they shine. You see the clouds, and you know that you are going up to them. You can't explain it—you just must get up there. You have a feeling that there is something there that you must go and see. Up you go, higher, higher, and higher into the sky around you.

Every step fills you with purpose. It reminds you that you are on the right track to that success that you are looking for. You take each step, knowing that you will get to where you need to go, little by little.

Soon, you make it to a layer of clouds. You stand there, looking at it for a moment. The clouds look fluffy soft all around you, plush, white, and inviting. You take the step onto them, and you are pleasantly surprised by the sensations surrounding you. Your feet feel softly embraced by the cloud's surface. You sink a little bit, but you can still feel that the cloud is firm enough to hold you up. It feels almost like walking on a large plush rug. The cloud squeezes between your toes as you walk, softly rubbing against your skin. It feels surprisingly warm, and for the first time, you realize that despite the fact that you are so high up in the sky that you can see your breath as you breathe, you are not cold at all.

In fact, you are grateful.

The sun in the sky bathes you in its golden hues, and you feel entirely content in the moment. You take a moment to bask in its warmth, and you keep walking forward. The clouds tickle as you walk, and soon, you realize that the stairs continue on up. You take another step, and this time, you manifest a stair made of the same plush cloud that you had just left behind. You keep walking, listening to the sound of your own breath, even and steady, and the soft whisper of the wind blowing around you as you continue your way. You feel ready for whatever will come next.

You are grateful for the chance to explore the world, and even beyond the world, as you continue to work your way up the stairs. Soon, you find yourself at the edge of it all. You step, and suddenly, you realize that you are no longer stepping on clouds.

You are now standing atop a massive plateau, built of stone. Strange, you tell yourself, you couldn't see the stone when you had been walking up. And, looking down, you don't seem to see anything beneath it. It is almost as if this strange, stony point is hovering there in the sky with you. You take a step onto it, expecting it to wobble. You brace yourself, but then you realize that it is perfectly still. It is not moving at all, and you are standing atop it without a care in the world. You are perfectly at home in the moment, and you know that where you are right that moment is where you were meant to be.

From your vantage point, the entirety of your world, of your imagination is visible. You can see endlessly, and you can see that your imagination is limitless. If you want to see something, you can manifest it here. You can think about what you want to see, and it will appear for you.

On one side, you can see a blanket of clouds expanding across the sky. It is slightly underneath your position. The clouds reflect the light of the gleaming sun and appear almost golden in their color as they sparkle brilliantly. You can see the surface of the clouds rippling, almost like waves of an ocean as the wind slowly carries and molds them. They ebb and flow, rotating and casting light shadows across their surfaces as they do. They look smooth and flow as they move.

Above you, you can see some thin, wispy clouds in the pale blue sky. The sun is higher now, and you can see the blue coming clear in the distance. The wisps of clouds move in their tiny little tufts, carried on air currents. They dance above you, flowing and caught in their own personal world away from your own.

You sit down on the rock surface under your feet, letting your legs dangle off the edge. You are miles above the ground, but you are unafraid. You know that you will not fall, and you know that you are safe. You sit there, watching the clouds move about, and you realize something: The clouds' rippling appears to be in response to your own breathing. With every breath that you exhale, you see what appears to be another wave, radiating out from the point where you are, rippling away from your location along the sky.

The sun above you sparkles and gleams, and though you are right in its light, you feel only warm. It is not too hot nor too cold.

You lean back on the rocks, and as you do so, you place your hands against their surfaces. They are just as smooth as the rocks that you had climbed up earlier, though these ones are darker and harder to get past. They are comfortable in your hand, and you feel at peace holding them where you do. You take in another breath, watching the beauty of your world. You feel at home.

As your hands rest on the ground, you feel something sprouting up around you. It is soft and almost warm, and when you look down, you are surprised to find that you are surrounded by grass and flowers. Little yellow flowers have popped up all around you, soft and inviting. You find yourself driven to follow them. You are pleased with how they feel, and as you look over your shoulder, you realize that the entire plateau is covered in the lush blanket of grass that spreads everywhere. That is the power of your inner peace and your mind. It creates softness and comfort wherever you go. It is self-compassion, creating a comfortable spot for you to land. Even when things are difficult, you can find yourself here. You can find yourself able to relax in the moment. You can feel comfortable where you are, and you can understand that even when you struggle, this inner peace is here for you.

As you breathe, you can hear the whispering of the grass rippling around you. You can feel it tickling, gently, with hundreds of blades, all along your hands and wrists. You can feel it wrapping you, supporting you, and relaxing you.

You feel yourself lay down in the grass, and it immediately feels like you are in the right spot. You feel like you could remain there forever. You watch as the clouds come and go above you. You can see them moving about above you in their little wisps, free and unburdened by anything. The clouds above you are utterly free and able to flow, and you can see them. You can see them moving throughout the sky as naturally as fish in water.

The sun grows lower, and you realize that you have been there far longer than you thought. You are suddenly laying there with the edges of the sky, starting to turn a faint purple with the vaguest hints of the impending twilight as the sun continues to set behind you.

Soon, the sky is alight with the sunset. It is burning brilliantly in streaks of reds and purple. It is brightly lit, filled up with pinks, and burning with oranges. It looks as if the entire sky were ablaze, and yet, the longer it lasted, the duller it grew, until finally, the entire sky faded into the darkness of night.

This time, the sky looks different. It is not the same, vast nothingness that you were in when you first arrived. The sky is dark, and yet it is filled with endless stars across its expanse. There is no moon, but that brings the brilliant pinpricks of light into even more view. You can see thousands upon thousands of them, more than you ever thought there were. They shimmer and flicker in the sky. Some of them look brighter than others. Some of them are closer to others.

A shooting star streaks across the sky almost leisurely, trailing behind it the long, white tail as it goes. It fills you with a moment of peace and calmness. Then, you see another shooting star, and another, until it looks like all of the stars are falling out of the sky. You can see them all, gently cascading around you. You can see them becoming visible, almost like glitter falling out of the sky.

Then, you realize that with every star that falls, your heart beats. Every little streak of light across the sky is a pump of your heart in your chest, calm, and content. You feel a concentrated warmth, right where that point in your center is. It is relaxing, almost heavily so. You can feel yourself sinking deeper into yourself and your mind. You can feel yourself growing more and more tired as you do so. You can feel yourself relaxing, fading away, and wishing for it to last.

You can feel the feelings of joy within yourself. You feel love for yourself and respect and kindness. You feel calm. You tell yourself that you are safe in this world. You are somewhere that you can be certain that you will be comfortable, and you have no worries. Any anxiety that you have is gone. It has been thrown with your tensions, leaving behind only the quiet, soft blanket of your peace of mind. All you feel is yourself within you. You feel at peace and at ease, and you are ready for yourself to remain right there. You get more comfortable and take a deep breath.

One... Two... Three... Four... Five...

And out...

One... Two... Three... Four... Five...

As you breathe deeper, you recognize that you are bringing yourself comfort. You feel sleepier. You feel ready to relax. You feel sleep starting to reach for you, and you welcome its embrace. Your whole body is

deeply relaxed as you watch the stars falling around
you to the rhythm of your heart.

You feel utterly calm in that moment, more than you
ever have before beneath those stars, in your own
personal paradise, nestled away from everything that
may have been bothering you. You are safe, and you
are so sleepy.

Across the sky, you see a great, big streak. It is silver,
shimmering, and it flies through the stars, leaving a
shimmering tail in its wake. You watch it, never taking
your eyes off of it. The shooting star itself fades away,
but you can still see the streak of its tail left across the
sky, spreading all the way across. You watch it, and it
looks almost shimmery as it is there. It remains right
there for you to see, and you watch it closely.

It's time for another deep breath in...

One... Two... Three... Four... Five...

And out...

One... Two... Three... Four... Five...

With every breath that you take, you see the streak in
the sky start to fade a little bit more. It slowly fades
out, first at the edges, until the edges are hazy and
beginning to blur. You feel perfectly at ease, and you
are ready to begin the bedtime story.

Guided Meditation 2: Counting Down to Sleep

Close your eyes and take in a big, deep breath. Feel the air flowing through your nose. Notice how it feels. Focus on the temperature and the smells. Feel it filling up your lungs, with your lungs swelling up within you like great, big balloons in your chest until you feel like they can't swell up anymore. Feel the air warming in your chest and exhale slowly, feeling the air pass your lips gently and slowly. Is it warm? With each breath that you take, you feel yourself calming down.

You breathe in... And out...

Now, feel yourself. Focus on your center, the point just above your belly button. How does it feel? Is it tense? Tight? Stressed? Focus on this point as you inhale in. One... Two... Three... Four... Five... and out... One... Two... three... Four... Five... Focus on that spot for another breath or two...

Now, feel the tension in your body. Become aware of any tension you are holding in your head and face. As you breathe in, imagine that you are pushing the tension down to the center above your belly button. Let it gather there. Now, feel the tension in your shoulders. Focus on that stress and tension and as you breathe in, feel it moving down to your center. Let it gather there, imagining your tension and stress all becoming balled up in the center. Feel the tension in your arms and hands gathering and flowing into your center. Feel that center growing with the tension and allow it to build up. Then, take the tension from your chest and upper back, and flow it down toward your center.

Then, go down to your toes and feet, identifying the tension that is there. Push it up, feeling it flowing up your legs, through your pelvis and belly, and noting it as it arrives in the belly. Focus on it as it grows within you and allow it to flow.

Feel all of the tension in your body, all boiled up into one big ball in your core. Allow yourself to feel the weight of that tension and the burden that it has been putting on you. Take in a deep breath as you focus on it. Then, bid it goodbye and goodnight.

As you exhale, pull the tension out from your core. Envision yourself picking up the ball of stress and tension and holding it like a basketball. Feel its heft in your mind. Inhale again. One... Two... Three... Four... Five... And as you exhale, throw the ball away from you. Watch as the ball of tension flies into the air. Watch it as it continues further and further away, getting smaller and smaller into the distance as you breathe. It is much smaller now and soon, it is so small that you can no longer see it, and then it is completely gone.

Now, in that space where you pulled the tension away, in your center, imagine that peace and calmness flows into you. It is slowly manifesting within your core, filling you with peace, comfort, and the feeling that everything will be okay. You have a big, shining silver ball of peace and relaxation within your core. Breathe in... One... Two... Three... Four... Five... And out... One... Two... Three... Four... Five... As you breathe in, imagine the feeling of relaxation extending throughout your body. Feel it in your head. Breathe in... and out... Feel the relaxation pulsating in your shoulders and arms... Feel it spreading throughout your chest. Feel it spread down to your legs and feet. It fills your whole body, bringing you utter peace and relaxation. Your mind feels incredibly open and ready to go on a peaceful, relaxing adventure. Your body is ready to fall deeper and deeper into your relaxation so you can become more and more relaxed.

With your core of relaxation, you can do anything that you want. You can fend off anxiety and worry. If you feel anxious in the moment, you can turn to the light of your inner center and have that guide you toward finding your inner success and peace. If you want to be able to ensure that you are at peace, you must first focus there. You must focus on what you want to be and how you can achieve it. If you want to be at total peace, you can be with ease. All you have to do is tap into that warm center that you have within yourself.

With your eyes still closed, relax your shoulders and chest. Let your stomach go lax. Breathe in deeply as you do so, allowing yourself to focus on the sensation within yourself. Tap into it closely, holding it close to yourself so that you can be certain that you are at total peace in the moment. Work to keep your mind nice and clear as you do so. Focus only on the sensation of your breathing and forego everything else. As you do this, you can feel your anxiety begin to fade away. Any anxiety that managed to remain in your body can be pushed away with this mindfulness. You focus solely on your breath.

You breathe in...

One... Two... Three... Four... Five...

And out...

One... Two... Three... Four... Five...

You breathe in...

One... Two... Three... Four... Five...

And out...

One... Two... Three... Four... Five...

Keep breathing until you start to feel more and more relaxed. You should notice that the anxiety starts to fade away. Now, it is time to count your way to sleep. With each breath, you must repeat to yourself these affirmations. You must say them as if you believe them, focusing on how they make you feel one by one. We will count down from 40 with each deep, long breath.

You breathe in...

One... Two... Three... Four... Five...

And out...

One... Two... Three... Four... Five...

We start at 40. You can see the number clearly in your mind as you sit there. You can feel it in your mind, and if you reached out, you knew you could touch it. You see fifty feathers, all floating around gently around you. Each feather helps to melt away your anxiety that you are feeling, and you say to yourself:

I did my best all day long, and I'm willing to forgive my shortfalls. I did enough, and I have no reason to feel anxious.

Now, we are at 39. Envision the curves of the 3 and the 9 in your mind, seeing them clearly. There are 39 flowers in your mind's eye, growing abundantly. They smell soft and sweet.

You breathe in...

One... Two... Three... Four... Five...

And out...

One... Two... Three... Four... Five...

I am supported. I am loved. I am safe. I am ready for a restful night of sleep.

38. You are calm as your breath fills your body. You can feel warmth emanating from your center, helping to push away the anxiety left over from a long day of stress around yourself.

You breathe in...

One... Two... Three... Four... Five...

And out...

One... Two... Three... Four... Five...

I feel completely at ease as I lay in bed, ready to sleep.

37. You can hear the sounds of 37 different birds, all chirping and singing to each other somewhere around you. The sound is melodic, almost hypnotic as it trills around you. The singing is beautiful, and with every note that you hear, you feel more and more at peace within yourself. Their song helps to create a beautiful melody within yourself that shields you from the anxiety that you feel.

You breathe in...

One... Two... Three... Four... Five...

And out...

One... Two... Three... Four... Five...

I will sleep deeply as I fall asleep. Insomnia will not keep me awake today.

36. The number 36 is round. You can see every single curve manifesting itself in your mind's eye. You can feel it within yourself. It is a square number. You see 36 apples, stacked up 6 by 6 in front of you, precariously balanced upon each other. However, they are perfectly stable. They are just as stable and secure as you are in your own mind right this moment.

You breathe in...

One... Two... Three... Four... Five...

And out...

One... Two... Three... Four... Five...

I can feel myself calmly drifting off to sleep as I count.

35. You look up into the sky. There are 35 clouds floating above you. You can get to know each one. They all look completely different than the others. They each have their own aspects within them to consider, to revere, to respect. When you see these, you realize that you are in a position where you can succeed in relaxing yourself. As the clouds drift past you, they take away your anxiety, leaving behind nothing but peace.

You breathe in...

One... Two... Three... Four... Five...

And out...

One... Two... Three... Four... Five...

Every night, I feel that sleeping is easier. It is more comfortable.

34. You are starting to feel sleepier as you go through this count. Now, you feel as if you can do whatever you may need to do in this world. You can see it within yourself so that you can relax. You can feel it within yourself. 34 waves of relaxation ripple across your body as you see the number in your mind.

You breathe in...

One... Two... Three... Four... Five...

And out...

One... Two... Three... Four... Five...

I can hear myself becoming calmer.

33. You are able to hear your calmness. It manifests in your breathing, slow and steady in your chest. You can hear the whispers of your breath into your nose and out of your mouth. You can hear it in your heart as it

beats slower and calmer. You can feel the peace coming within you as 33 autumn leaves gently drift past you on a soft breeze.

You breathe in...

One... Two... Three... Four... Five...

And out...

One... Two... Three... Four... Five...

I will naturally fall asleep as I count down.

32. With the manifestation of 32 in your mind, you can notice your attention drifting. It wants to wander. Your thoughts want to slip away... And you pull it back to your counting. You focus your mind on your breathing.

You breathe in...

One... Two... Three... Four... Five...

And out...

One... Two... Three... Four... Five...

I can feel myself calming down, and I will always calm down in the evening as bedtime comes closer

31. You feel pleasantly calm in the moment. You are enjoying the stillness that reminds you that things can

be calm. Things can be safe and comfortable. You can
be at ease here, in your bed. You can see 31 small, soft
white moths fluttering about around you, peacefully
keeping themselves just barely aloft with their wings.
They look beautiful, reflecting moonlight so brilliantly
that they look like they might glow.

You breathe in...

One... Two... Three... Four... Five...

And out...

One... Two... Three... Four... Five...

*I am relaxed and at peace in the moment, and even if
I am not asleep, I am relaxed.*

30. You can feel yourself feeling warm in your bed.
You settle down deeper, nestling down into the perfect
comfortable spot, and embrace it. This is the best you
have felt in a long while... peacefully content with the
world around you. You hear the sounds of 30 crickets
quietly chirping outside of your room.

You breathe in...

One... Two... Three... Four... Five...

And out...

One... Two... Three... Four... Five...

I deserve to be relaxed.

29. You focus on the sensation of sleep. What is sleep? Sleep is when you drift away. You focus on that hazy in-between where you are not quite asleep but not quite awake, inviting it to come into yourself to guide you off to sleep. You can do it as you hear the soft rustling of your sheets underneath you.

You breathe in...

One... Two... Three... Four... Five...

And out...

One... Two... Three... Four... Five...

I deserve to get a full night of restful sleep.

28. You allow yourself to drift in your mind. You tell yourself that sleep is possible. You allow yourself to sort of float on that halfway between conscious and unconscious. You feel perfectly at ease.

You breathe in...

One... Two... Three... Four... Five...

And out...

One... Two... Three... Four... Five...

I can sleep all night long and still wake up refreshed.
I deserve it.

27. You feel pleasant where you are. You focus on the numbers as you continue to count them. Just saying the number is enough to invite another wave of inner peace to you that you can use to help yourself find that point of sleep. The more that you do this, the closer to sleep you feel.

You breathe in...

One... Two... Three... Four... Five...

And out...

One... Two... Three... Four... Five...

I release everything that happened today, and I am no longer worried about what I cannot change.

26. You can hear your body relaxing. Your feet feel pleasantly heavy, sinking deeper into your bed. You cannot bear to move them as you sit there, enjoying the comfort that they bring. You stay there for yourself, focusing on what you can do to better comfort yourself.

You breathe in...

One... Two... Three... Four... Five...

And out...

One... Two... Three... Four... Five...

I am thankful for what I did today.

25. As you think about 25, you feel calm. You feel thankful for the day that you have and for every aspect of it. Every moment was valuable for you, and you genuinely appreciate it. Imagine the best part of your day for a moment, focusing immensely on it as you sit there in your mind. Relive that moment of calm quiet that you loved. Focus on how wonderful it was and how happy and grateful you are that you can move forward tomorrow as well, loved, happy, and well-rested.

You breathe in...

One... Two... Three... Four... Five...

And out...

One... Two... Three... Four... Five...

Sleep is natural, and my body knows exactly how to get me to that point.

24. You can see 24 stars above where you are. They are twinkling and glistening above you. They shimmer and shine. They dance and move. They are beautiful. You feel in awe of the and of the world that they exist in. You marvel at the wonders of the universe and feel so glad to be a part of it.

You breathe in...

One... Two... Three... Four... Five...

And out...

One... Two... Three... Four... Five...

I am allowed to have a sleep that is restful and complete.

23. You feel better now. Your body is entirely at ease. Now, you must help your mind find that inner peace as well, one step at a time. You hear your thoughts, one by one, dancing around you. They are getting louder and louder... Your doubts and fears... And one by one, you silence them. You let them drift away from you so that you can get back to your clarity and peace.

You breathe in...

One... Two... Three... Four... Five...

And out...

One... Two... Three... Four... Five...

I can fall asleep whenever I am ready and whenever I choose to do so.

22. You can feel that your body is ready to sleep, but your mind is still doubting. Gently, you remind your mind that everything that happened today happened for a reason, even if you do not understand it. You let go of the things that you don't understand, and you

remind yourself that you can successfully get through your life, one night at a time.

You breathe in...

One... Two... Three... Four... Five...

And out...

One... Two... Three... Four... Five...

My sleep and my dreams will be peaceful.

21. Your mind is starting to slow down now... It still has some stirrings of doubt, of anxiety, of worry... But you know in your heart that things will be okay. You know that you can create the life that you want to live, and that begins with a night of good sleep.

You breathe in...

One... Two... Three... Four... Five...

And out...

One... Two... Three... Four... Five...

I am in control of how I sleep.

20. You remind yourself that you are what you attract. If you want restful sleep, you must project out that you are open to restful sleep, and you must genuinely open up your mind to it. When you open up your

mind to the peace within yourself, you know that you can bring in that peaceful night's sleep.

You breathe in...

One... Two... Three... Four... Five...

And out...

One... Two... Three... Four... Five...

I sleep soundly.

19. The more that you focus on your sleep, the more inviting it becomes. You feel the need for sleep growing stronger... Heavier... More compelling. Your body is starting to feel far away as you continue to breathe and relax.

You breathe in...

One... Two... Three... Four... Five...

And out...

One... Two... Three... Four... Five...

I can feel myself falling asleep.

18. You are getting closer than ever to falling asleep, and you welcome and embrace it. You are happy to have that sleep coming your way, and all you must do is welcome it into your own life. If you want that peace

and solitude, all you have to do is remind yourself that you can achieve it.

You breathe in...

One... Two... Three... Four... Five...

And out...

One... Two... Three... Four... Five...

I can feel my muscles relaxing.

17. Your whole body feels so far away that you feel like you are going to float away. You can see yourself in your mind's eye, resting comfortably and in total relaxation. You can see that there are no dangers here. You are in your own home, within your own walls, and able to get the rest that you are looking for.

You breathe in...

One... Two... Three... Four... Five...

And out...

One... Two... Three... Four... Five...

I can feel my eyes getting heavy.

16. You surround yourself in your mind with the peace and serenity you need. It slowly comes toward you, a peaceful, soft light that engulfs your whole body. You can see that you have a haze of light surrounding you,

basking you in a faint silvery light. This light is your protection. It will help you to sleep.

You breathe in...

One... Two... Three... Four... Five...

And out...

One... Two... Three... Four... Five...

I am happy to be here, ready for sleep.

15. You tell yourself that the light around you is your barrier between the world and yourself. It will help you to keep the negative thoughts out of your mind, allowing only the positive thoughts into yourself so you can begin to relax and enjoy a night without worrying about burdening yourself or being unable to sleep. You focus on just how happy and content you are in the moment. You are perfectly relaxed, and you are happier than ever.

You breathe in...

One... Two... Three... Four... Five...

And out...

One... Two... Three... Four... Five...

My dreams will be full of just as much serenity as I am right now, counting.

14. You think about your most perfect dream. You can
see it in your mind's eye, and you focus intently on it.
You can bring it to fruition. The more you focus on it,
the more likely that you are to sleep and dream it.

You breathe in...

One... Two... Three... Four... Five...

And out...

One... Two... Three... Four... Five...

My head feels heavy as I rest it.

13. You are so tired that you can barely stand it any
longer. You can't keep up with fighting it off any
longer. You can't keep yourself awake any longer in
your current state, and you know that... So you make
the decision to let sleep overcome you.

You breathe in...

One... Two... Three... Four... Five...

And out...

One... Two... Three... Four... Five...

*My sleep will heal my body so I can feel better and
ready to take on the day.*

12. You remind yourself of all of the wonderful
benefits that you manifest when you are able to sleep

at night. You know that your body will heal. You imagine there being great, big, healing waves flowing over your body, following your willingness to sleep.

You breathe in...

One... Two... Three... Four... Five...

And out...

One... Two... Three... Four... Five...

I am a heavy sleeper, and I will be able to sleep, even if there is some noise.

11. You imagine yourself sleeping all night long, waking up the next morning in total peace and comfort. You remind yourself that you can get yourself there. You just have to keep focusing and allow the sleep to take over.

You breathe in...

One... Two... Three... Four... Five...

And out...

One... Two... Three... Four... Five...

I'm ready to let go of my anxiety and the insomnia that comes with it.

10. You know that the sleep is going to take you over, and you are welcoming it.

You breathe in...

One... Two... Three... Four... Five...

And out...

One... Two... Three... Four... Five...

I'm ready to fall asleep deeply.

9. You can hear your breathing shifting again. It is even slower and deeper. It is peaceful. You are at peace.

You breathe in...

One... Two... Three... Four... Five...

And out...

One... Two... Three... Four... Five...

My body is open to a complete, relaxing state where I can sleep.

8. You can feel yourself getting so close to sleeping. The more that you focus on the sleep, the more that you want it. You can imagine yourself sleeping. You can see your cells within your body healing

themselves, becoming more capable of getting through to you. You can feel yourself relaxing more and more... And you are ready to embrace it.

You breathe in...

One... Two... Three... Four... Five...

And out...

One... Two... Three... Four... Five...

I release the negativity and negative energy within myself.

7. The negative thoughts that have bothered you all night long are rejected. There is no reason for your anxiety to rule you any longer. You should not allow those thoughts to hold you back or prevent you from success. You can do this. You just have to embrace it.

You breathe in...

One... Two... Three... Four... Five...

And out...

One... Two... Three... Four... Five...

My bedroom is my sanctuary; my point of peace and relaxation. It is my place I can truly be at home.

6. You take that silvery light that was shining around you, and you feel it expand around your entire bedroom. It shields you. It protects you. It prevents you from giving in to the negativity in the world while also shielding you from the negativity that exists out there as well. You can fend it off this way. You can thrive and survive.

You breathe in...

One... Two... Three... Four... Five...

And out...

One... Two... Three... Four... Five...

I am worthy of that stress-free sleep that I will achieve.

5. You remind yourself that you deserve sleep. Everyone deserves sleep just as much as everyone deserves food, warmth, and love. Sleep is essential, and you deserve to get a good, peaceful night's rest within yourself. You deserve to feel good, to feel content, and to feel in total love with yourself. You deserve to get that sleep, and you are the only one that can give it to yourself.

You breathe in...

One... Two... Three... Four... Five...

And out...

One... Two... Three... Four... Five...

As I sleep, I will attract more success and peace tomorrow.

4. You remind yourself that your sleep will help you. You have no reason to sacrifice it to try to force through other things. You deserve to rest. You need to rest. You will rest.

You breathe in...

One... Two... Three... Four... Five...

And out...

One... Two... Three... Four... Five...
I know that my insomnia is interfering with my sleep, but I will reject it. I release it back into the world. I am ready and open to sleep.

3. You are so close now... you can barely even think. You can barely even focus on your breathing within your chest. You are ready to give in completely. And you do.

You breathe in...

One... Two... Three... Four... Five...

And out...

One... Two... Three... Four... Five...

My body is awake during the day, so it can sleep at night.

2. You give in to the need to sleep, and you will thank yourself tomorrow for it.

You breathe in...

One... Two... Three... Four... Five...

And out...

One... Two... Three... Four... Five...

I will wake up to my alarm clock, awake, and ready to go.

1. You are ready. You are asleep. You are at total peace without an ounce of anxiety left in you.

You breathe in...

One... Two... Three... Four... Five...

And out...

One... Two... Three... Four... Five...

I am now ready to sleep entirely. My body is perfectly relaxed and ready. My mind is at peace. My heart is happy. Good night, sleep well. Rest peacefully.

Description

Bedtime stories aren't just for kids anymore...

Do you find that you suffer from insomnia, no matter how hard you try to cope with it? Are you always exhausted even though you know that you shouldn't be? If you find that bedtime is impossible for you to cope with, then this book is for you!

As you read through this book, you will be introduced to the idea of using stories and mindfulness to help yourself drift off to sleep. There is a reason that bedtime stories are so recommended for getting children to sleep. After all—having time to enjoy a story allows your mind to relax and allows you to begin to focus more on the moment. As you listen to bedtime stories, or as you read them, you are able to feel at peace. You can allow your mind to focus on those details that you might not otherwise be able to. You will find that being able to enjoy a story will help your mind relax and grant you that ability to sleep.

In this book, you will first be introduced to the idea of mindful meditation so you can begin to understand just how powerful it can be. Then, you will be provided with several options for bedtime stories. Each story is designed to be a calming slice of life story about the various adventures (and sometimes misadventures) of Sophie Rogers, a young woman that lives in the Pacific Northwest with her German shepherd pal, Bella. Together, and sometimes separately, they get out and enjoy their lives, and the stories of her day to day life can help you to relax and soothe yourself into a state in which you will be able to relax. As you read, you should find yourself calming down and preparing for a night of sleep. Each of the options that are provided to you should be fun and engaging without keeping you up at night.

Finally, at the end of the book, you will be given two more traditional mindful meditations that are designed to trigger that state of mindfulness within yourself so you can then begin to relax and enjoy a restful night's sleep. When you learn to use these various techniques, you can work with yourself to ensure that you can calm yourself down when you need to, allowing yourself to get that relaxation that you need.

If you're ready to start sleeping better, then you are in the right spot. This book may be able to help you relax enough to fall asleep! As you read, you can expect to see:

- An adventure in which Sophie and Bella go hiking and get lost in the mountains
- A rush for Sophie and her best friend, Cara, to get to the airport in time for their vacation to Greece that teaches them a valuable lesson
- A tour through the Acropolis of Athens, the place of Sophie's dreams
- A trip through a beautiful mansion as Cara tries to buy a house in the area and tours some of the nicest areas that town has to offer

- A story in which Sophie runs into her old roommate from college and catches up with her
- A misadventure through the mall where Sophie tries something new and learns not to trust all of the different activities and ideas suggested on the internet
- Two guided meditations to help you fall asleep with ease

If you're ready to fall asleep, then don't let another day pass you buy. Enjoy these stories and see if sleep is more within your grasp than you realized!

www.ingramcontent.com/pod-product-compliance
Lightning Source LLC
Chambersburg PA
CBHW071532100726
47908CB00004B/1374